LOCKED TOGETHER

A singer-songwriter-scientist from the North of England takes his first steps in love in the late sixties

MIKE WHITAKER

Copyright © 2021 Mike Whitaker

All rights reserved. No part of this book may be reproduced or utilized in any form or by any means, electronic or mechanical, including photocopying, recording or by any information storage or retrieval system, without permission in writing from the Publisher, except in the case of brief quotations embodied in critical reviews and certain other non-commercial uses permitted by law. Inquiries should be addressed to the Permissions Department via tomwhitakerbooks@gmail.com

ISBN: 9798781732777

DEDICATION

With much love to my wife Carol for her encouragement
and support during the production of this book.

CONTENTS

Acknowledgments	i
Chapter One	1
Chapter Two	21
Chapter Three	49
Chapter Four	89
Chapter Five	111
Chapter Six	169
Chapter Seven	189

ACKNOWLEDGMENTS

Special thanks to my son for his encouragement to complete this book and his incisive comments during the final stages of editing.

PART ONE

CHAPTER ONE

By taking a left turn instead of a right I had found myself at the top end of the road. Looking down I could see where the house was probably situated. It was to be number 38 and a solitary car parked on the road probably marked the spot. The weather was distinctly inclement; grey and misty with a pervading feeling of dampness. It had permeated my coat and I could feel the chill of wetness against my neck as I tried, with one hand, to button up my coat collar. The evening was drawing in. I put down one of my cases so I could reach for the full address. Mrs. Carter, Number 38, Denver Street, West Hampstead, London.

This was only my second time in London. It was 1966 and my University life was about to begin. I took in a deep breath as though these bleak, undistinguished surroundings were somehow to unleash a magical adventure, something special, never before experienced. Of course, it wouldn't. I knew that. But London in the mid-sixties was a special place. There was a sense of optimism, an innocent excitement that only the youthful can possess. I was poised, ready to meet the challenges. Or so I thought. What I should have felt was quite something else, because as we all know, what lay down that road and beyond required more, much more.

I picked up the cases and strode purposely towards the area where the car was parked. The dark silhouette of an old Edwardian house began to take shape. At the same time from out of the house came several shadowy figures. They shouted to each other with a heavy distinctive accent. As I got closer the shape of four young men became clearer as they scrambled into a car. The car pulled away into the gloom. I turned to approach the doorway. I was correct. This was indeed number 38. I knocked on the heavy wooden door. After no response I tried twice again, this time with the iron door knocker, which was considerably louder and more effective. The door finally opened to reveal a rather tiny, older woman with silvery hair. She looked annoyed.

"There is a doorbell you know! Why don't you use it!" she shouted sharply.

"I'm sorr….." I began but she interrupted.

"Come on in, if you're coming in," she said sternly again. "Which one are you? I'm expecting four of you. Where are the others?" I could see she didn't really want an answer. She just wanted to shout, or so it seemed, at me.

"I thought those people who have just left might have been them," I suggested tentatively.

"Not at all, that was my husband and that new, fangled group….Oh what are they called?" She was irritated again, as she struggled to concentrate. And then with a more satisfied expression she mumbled "Oh I remember now….They call themselves the Beatles…..Or is it the Beatniks?"

"The Beatles," I repeated. I paused for a moment and then said again, "The Beatles…you mean they really were the

Beatles?" How could she say this so calmly? My favorite group; my idols; everyone's idols, ….here! I had missed them. A matter of seconds and I would have met them. "That accent, of course I recognized that accent. And the way they moved ….I knew it, I knew it." I was beginning to feel angry now that I didn't move just that fraction quicker. One of them had looked out of the window as they drove away, his face up against the glass. "It could easily have been Paul," I thought.

"Who was this person, an old lady, in the middle of nowhere who knows The Beatles?"

"Are you sure it was the Beatles?" I was trying to keep her attention.

"Oh yes, I'm quite sure," she said harshly and began to climb the stairs. "He's taking them to the Palladium, and he won't be back until tomorrow, if I see him at all this week."

I picked up my things and began to follow her. With the minimum of words, she pointed out my room and the bathroom and then disappeared downstairs. I turned and then lay on the bed. I lay there staring at the ceiling, wondering at what just happened and wishing I had just been ten seconds earlier.

The room had a musty feel about it. With no heating it was distinctly cold. Feeling as I did, I simply got under the covers to keep warm and began to stare at the ceiling again. The next thing I knew, I was being woken by a voice urging me to get up.

"It's breakfast time. I think you should get up." I opened my eyes to see a face grinning down at me. "I'm Gary, I arrived last night. I don't think we should keep Mrs. Carter waiting." He had a roundish sort of face but friendly. His voice sounded a little posh and I immediately noticed his dark long hair was swept back giving him an older, almost parental appearance.

"Isn't it Sunday?" I asked weakly.

"Yes, but I think we should go down now for breakfast. She's expecting us." His tone was more insistent.

I briefly glanced around at the unfamiliar room. Pulling back the bed clothes, I suddenly realised that I had slept fully clothed.

"Cold were you last night," he said smiling.

"It's still cold," I said trying to pull the bed clothes back again. "My name's Nick," I was embarrassed by the state of my clothes. "Are you staying here as well?…Have any of the others arrived?" He was, and the others hadn't arrived as far as he knew. We had breakfast, served by a displeased looking Mrs. Carter and then chatted together for a while at the table. He was going to do a physics degree.

"I always wanted to do physics or even geology….I like to know how everything works," I said wistfully. "Instead I'm doing geography."

"Physics can be pretty boring. Actually, I'd rather be in business like my father." He sounded disappointed.

Mrs. Carter came in and without a word began to clear away. We moved out of the way to be accommodating. She still didn't look pleased.

"Can we help?" said Gary politely. Again, not a word. Gary

gave me a warped smile as if to say, "What is the problem!" She left the room.

"Would you believe that woman entertained the Beatles here in this house yesterday," I said wryly.

"Yeah sure, and Elvis gets his breakfast here as well." chuckled Gary incredulously. He didn't believe me but before I could tell him more, he suddenly noticed the time and said he had to leave. There was no more time to chat. Left alone I decided to make my way to college and acquaint myself with the place. As I walked towards the front door, the doorbell rang. Without a word Mrs. Carter pushed passed me to open the door. A familiar voice rang out.
"Hello Mrs. Carter, it's me again"
The voice sounded very familiar.
"It couldn't be," I mumbled. But it was ……Cliff Richard. I was so surprised.

"I've come for my breakfast!"
He quickly took off his coat, which curiously, had fur linings along the edges.

"Very trendy" I was thinking.

Unbelievably, he was now standing directly in front of me. I was thinking "What is this place? What is going on here?"

"I'm so sorry, it seems I'm getting in your way." I mumbled.

"Don't worry" he said calmly, "I'm not in a hurry today, thank goodness."

Mrs. Carter turned and went down the narrow passageway

to the kitchen. He then turned towards me.

"And who are you?"
"Wow," I thought "He actually wants to speak to me!"
"I'm just a student at Bedford College in Regents Park."
"Mrs. Carter looking after you?" he enquired.
"Of course," afraid to say any more. "Do you stay here often?"

"Yes, Mrs. Carter provides an anonymous base for many of us in show business. I suppose you are surprised by all this." I sensed he must have noticed my wide eyed stare. He continued.

"Her husband Paul looks after the transportation. It's so we can get to our venues on time and avoid any issues with screaming fans."

"That explains why the Beatles were here. I saw them leave yesterday evening."
"Oh really. And now you are left with just me" He smiled.
"Anyway, nice to meet you but you will have to excuse me, I need one of Mrs. Carter's king size cups of tea." With that he turned to go and disappeared into the kitchen.

"Wow" I thought, "Who will believe this when I tell them?"

My thoughts were then obliged to turn to the more mundane thoughts of college. I looked forward to the journey and the novelty of using the Tube. It was a short walk to the tube station. I bought my ticket and climbed the stairs to the platform, which seemed strange since this was supposed to be part of the Underground. A train soon followed and with a loud squeak pulled to a halt. The doors slid open and I entered to find the carriage virtually empty. I sat on a rather ancient seat and surveyed the scene.

"So this was the renowned Bakerloo Line." I had heard so much about this famous line that it felt like I was experiencing a part of history. The few other passengers sat motionless in their seats, unmoved by the occasion as we rattled very noisily towards Baker Street. It was then only a short walk to the university. I had waited a long time for this moment.

London University was, in fact, a very large university made up loosely of several colleges located in and around the city and I had found myself a place here, at Bedford College and now I was finally here.

I looked up expectantly at the tall iron gates. I stared at the outside of the building, savouring every moment as I stood before these hallowed walls. It was suitably impressive and fitted the image I had created of what a university should look like. I liked that. Built in the nineteenth century it had a well proportioned classical appearance made up of predominantly red brick, but tastefully finished with Georgian windows and palisades. It was also idyllically set within a park, Regents Park in fact, hidden away from the hustle and bustle of the real London. A sanctuary of calm and greenery despite the threatening skyline of Victorian and Georgian rooftops laying siege around the perimeter.

I pushed on one of the heavy gates. They were closed. I leaned against them again. One of them yielded a few inches. I tried once more, and this time with force. It opened. I was pleased and walked the short distance to the main entrance. On entering, an echoey hollow sound greeted me as I strode down towards, what appeared to be, the refectory. I paused at the end of a dark corridor. A sign indicated 'Geography Department'. I listened for indications of life. Again, there was no sound and so unlikely anyone was there. Disappointingly, it seemed I was alone and began to wonder if I should actually be here.

I walked on, down the corridor and entered one of the laboratories. A single student sat intently reading at the far corner of the room. I decided not to disturb him, said a quick hello and left. I paused again to listen out for signs of activity. There was nothing.

A department notice board caught my attention and in the half light of the gloom I eagerly tried to read it. There was nothing of interest, nothing that I could understand. It all related to the previous term. I continued on, down to the refectory and then on to a coffee lounge area. No one, everywhere seemed deserted. A few old magazines lay discarded on the easy chairs in the lounge but no signs of life. I stared out through the French windows at the damp weather outside and wondered what to do next. There seemed little choice. An old upright piano sat invitingly in the corner of the room. It was well used and a little out of tune. Since I was keen on playing the piano and there was no one to disturb I spent the next few hours quite happily in the key of F major.

By the time I had finished playing it was getting late. There were no lights and it was dark. I decided to make my way back to the digs, stopping off at the tube station café at Baker Street for a plate of baked beans on toast. This would be my meal for the evening. Back at the digs there were three new arrivals…one more than I had expected.

It seemed I was sharing my bedroom with Andy Milner, a Cornishman and, as I entered the room, he was in the orderly process of unpacking. My cases still lay untouched at the side of the bed. After exchanging names, he returned to his business of unpacking.

"It's quite cold in here," I ventured.

"It doesn't worry me," came a curt response. He continued unpacking. I watched him take each item, one by one, set them out in piles before hanging them carefully in the wardrobe.

"I actually slept fully clothed last night," I ventured again.

"I can see that," he replied without looking up. "Not the healthiest thing to do."

"Not the best thing to do," copying his same negative tone.

"What do you do?" He didn't answer. Not straight away. He first finished setting up his pajamas on the pillow after turning down the bed sheets.

"English," he suddenly said. The conversation ceased again.

I placed one of my cases on the bed wondering if I should mention the Beatles but thought better of it. For some reason he still wasn't prepared to make any attempt at conversation.

"Do you have any special interests other than English?" I asked hesitantly, thinking at the same time that for an English student, he didn't seem to use very much of it. This was definitely my last attempt at the introductions. I was beginning to irritate myself.

"I like to sing," An encouraging remark, especially since I had my guitar.

"Really, so do I," I spoke enthusiastically, too

enthusiastically considering his previous reticence. Still this sounded promising.

"My favorite music is opera," he began. "I have a repertoire of English Madrigals but have recently specialised in eighteenth century folksongs." This did not sound like me. Now I was speechless. I couldn't match that. At least I was right not to mention the Beatles visit. I stepped outside to visit the bathroom. On the short landing I met another of the new residents.

"Hello, I'm Brian!" he said spritely. "I'm waiting for Aaron to come out. He's been in there ages."

"Are you also going to Bedford?"

"Yes, to do history. I'm rather looking forward to it."

He seemed an amiable person. At least he smiled. He was a little plump and had large round black rimmed spectacles with short black hair which gave him a sort of young schoolboy appearance.

"It doesn't look like ……" I paused because I couldn't remember the name.

"Aaron," added Brian helpfully.
"……Aaron is coming out," I said finally, "Do you think he's ok? Perhaps you should knock on the door? Perhaps he needs help?"

"I think I'll go and read a little," said Brian, side stepping the matter, and then disappeared into his room. I decided to do the same. As I sat on the bed Andy passed by me with a towel also on the way to the bathroom. I heard the door open and the sound of footsteps. After a few minutes he returned.

"Is the bathroom free now?" I asked.

"For residents it is," quipped Andy. I was taken aback.

The next morning I arose and went down to breakfast, quickly followed by the others. Aaron was already there, sat at the table. I was immediately struck by his long gaunt pale face, long neck and basin cropped dark but straggly hair. One by one we each said hello as we sat down. There was a pause as we naturally awaited Aaron's response. At first nothing. Then without movement of the head he rolled his eyes eerily and stared at us in turn. Staring straight ahead he spoke slowly and deliberately with a strange, nasal sound partly created by the fact his jaw barely moved. It was very odd.

"Which of you seemed to think I needed help last night?" he cackled. I looked over at Gary who seemed equally perplexed. Nobody answered. Aaron then suddenly shifted his stare directly at me. Continuing this stare he crackled again using the same strange voice. "Nobody here then…….how unusual." He managed a forced grin which he held as he screwed his eyes to peer accusingly at us. Fortunately, Mrs. Carter entered the room with four very greasy plates of egg and bacon. This attracted a lot of comment from Gary and to my relief normal conversation was resumed.

Breakfast over, I prepared myself for college. Today would be registration day and I needed to bring with me the necessary documentation. A simple task one might think but, in my case, holding on to important papers was never straight forward. I peered into my suitcase and tried to concentrate on which papers I should need. As per usual I couldn't think straight, the anticipation of the day ahead blurring my thoughts. I decided to take them all. I quickly closed the case, grabbed my coat and bag and ran downstairs, deliberately avoiding Aaron on the way. Gary was nowhere to be seen so I made my own way to the station.

It was a typical cold and wet October morning. I ran the last hundred yards towards the gates partly in excitement and partly to avoid a soaking. I entered through the main doors and then paused to check the state of my clothes. A hum of voices filled the air. There were people everywhere. The main hallway, which was so empty and hollow yesterday, was now filled with a real buzz of excitement. A new term had begun. I surveyed the sea of faces and immediately noticed how many were female. I don't think, I'd seen so many before in one place. Tables lined both sides of the hallway covered in leaflets with all kinds of information about college societies, charity groups, sport activities, social events. It was very noisy, a marketplace atmosphere. A rather attractive girl shouted out to me to come and join the Philately Society. I was tempted but uppermost in my mind was registration and the need to feel securely established. Reluctantly I turned away and made my way towards the Geography Department. On the way I had to pass the Geology Department and wistfully observed the small group of students waiting to register. "This is a subject I'd much rather do." I thought. But all my previous attempts had been turned down.

On reaching Geography I was surprised to see the long queue of students lined up along the full length of the corridor. To my horror, at the head of the line stood the gangly figure of Aaron. He had the same odd expression and seemed to stand awkwardly as he defended his leading position at the front of the queue. "God, three years of Aaron" My heart sank. Prompted by this unwelcome vision I decided then and there to go back to the Geology queue and chance my luck. One last attempt. It appeared there would be ample time. Aaron had given me an added incentive now.

Amazingly it took no effort at all. When I returned to the Geology Department, I was able to walk straight into the office to meet a Dr. Bridgstone who immediately accepted my application. She was almost keen; most unusual. Perhaps this year was undersubscribed. Whatever the reason I was now doing a subject I really wanted to do. What luck! I felt really pleased with myself. I stepped outside and surveyed the corridor. I was finally here, where I'd wanted to be. I'd arrived.

The next few weeks were hectic. I'd never really experienced the lecture system and it took some getting used to. Nevertheless, a routine began to emerge. Relations with Aaron did not improve, but I had met with many others who seemed more amenable.

College life provided a readymade social life; the opportunity to meet people from different backgrounds with different ideas. One such person was Peter Fisher. He was a significant character in the Geology class. He came up with a zany new idea every day, which was great, although it was often difficult to take him seriously. Peter was a narrow-faced sort of person with an angular chin covered by a small wispy thin beard. He was very conspicuous for his black rimmed, thick lensed spectacles. Despite his rather gangly appearance he was also conspicuous for the rather pretty young lady to whom he was about to be engaged. She was not part of the college and I only rarely saw them together. He had an exceptionally engaging sense of humor and outgoing personality which usually placed him center stage wherever he went. At the same time, he could steer an entertaining conversation into some interesting subject areas raising very pertinent philosophical conundrums and observations. It was during a coffee break in those early days that a particular discussion first evolved around the concept of the word 'selfish'.

As I sat at the table, Peter placed two coffees down and pushed a half-filled cup towards me. He sat down looking straight at me with a mock grin across his face, as I stared accusingly at his full cup of coffee. He awaited a response.

"A selfish pig, you are Peter," I said, trying not to smile.

"I know," he said proudly.

"I don't know how that fiancée of yours puts up with you," I suggested.

"She knows," he said again proudly.

"I bet she does,"

"Of course she does. Everything I do is selfish," he confirmed, emphasizing the words "Everything" and "Selfish". The way he emphasised these words was clearly intended. They rang loudly in my head. The thought that "everything" was selfish somehow appealed. It had a sort of warped truth about it.

"What do you mean by that?" Knowing that he wanted me to ask.

"I know everything I do is selfish," he repeated. "And everything you do is".

This was music to my ears. I didn't realize at that moment all its implications but I could feel my hair beginning to stand on end as this small phrase, this small seed, began to grow inside my head. I just knew it was true and that this tiny, little phrase was fundamental.

Peter continued to explain that he was a member of Mensa, a privileged group of people recognised for their high IQ's. The society was formed to string together like-minded persons with high IQ's and to promote the development of intellectual pursuit. One of the members had suggested Selfishness as a notion to discuss for their next meeting.

"You mean everything I do - walking, talking and sleeping?" I asked.

"Yep," he replied smugly.

"Even helping people?"

"Yep," came again the smug response.

I loved this. I knew it was true, I was catching on fast and wanted to challenge and test every aspect of such a hypothesis. But I couldn't. By this time, we had been joined by Steve Langley and James Granger, two other course mates, who immediately picked up our coffees and drank them. They were not popular.

It wasn't until the next day during an ill-fated biology practical that I would discuss this idea again. Steve Langley, a very likable yet still outgoing character (that is when he wasn't stealing my coffee), sat at the side of me as we stared down at the sacrifices before us. We each had a rabbit to dissect. They were all domestically bred and lay there as perfect fluffy and cuddly specimens, with the exception of course, that they were dead. The exercise began by spreading the arms and legs wide to the side and prizing them down to a board with skewers. This was not that easy, but it did expose the full chest and body area ready for incision. We were instructed to make a long cut down the middle chest area and to pull the skin layers to each side. It was a rather gruesome procedure. I turned towards Steve. He was concentrated on the dissection and bent over, his long wavy dark hair hanging down covering his face and the rabbit. I tried to attract his attention.

"Have you heard about this selfish idea from Peter at all?"

"Yer what?" he said with a demonic tone as he deliberately turned his head menacingly towards me. His pale sultry face together with the long hair gave him the look of someone between Jesus and Rasputin. He maintained the pretense of the demonic pose whilst he licked his lips noisily and began in a gravelly voice most comparable to Long John Silver,

"Yer must excuse me, yer see I haven't 'ad mi breakfast yet. It's not every day yer get fresh meat."

He was very convincing, and I had to laugh.

"You're 'orrible," trying not to think about it.

"You should eat more fiber," I instructed.

"Yeah I do, I like those shredded.....er.." He paused to think of the name.

"Shredded Wheat?" I suggested.

"No, no," he said continuing his ol'sea faring accent.

"Pussycats... shredded pussycats, that's what I like."

We continued with more incisions until surface muscles had been removed leaving some of the vital organs exposed. The rabbit was still curiously warm having only recently, that morning, been gassed for the purpose of the practical.

"Changing the subject Steve, did you catch any of that discussion with Peter, you know about selfishness?"

Steve's voice returned to normal, a London accent derived from the Guildford area.

"I think it's important. I just know it is," hoping he would keep a serious tone. I continued.

"It means everything we do is selfish, not only the nasty things but even the most charitable".

He was still looking at me, so I persevered.

Everything we do in our life, literally everything is selfish and with a capital 'S'. Why?....Because I think it links with the Darwinian concepts of survival".

"Survival of the fittest," suggested Steve thoughtfully.

"In other words, everything we do is for our own survival and so it is inevitable that everything we do is for our purely selfish needs," I said with enthusiasm. Steve picked up on this.

"So you're saying that when we eat and drink that's selfish because we're doing this purely to enable us to survive?"

I agreed.

"What about if you give money to someone - how can that be selfish?" asked Steve.

"Because in some way, giving that money will help you," I replied confidently.

"How?" he said disbelievingly.

"Hoarding your money only makes you unpopular. People get angry. Giving pacifies; it's an insurance policy, a survival strategy. Just take the French Revolution as an example and you get the idea of what can happen if you don't give.

"I see," said Steve suspiciously, "So when I helped you out with that money the other day, it was me who was being selfish?" said Steve inquisitively.

"Yep," I said with certainty.

"So, it would be very unselfish of me to ask for it back," Steve had a big smile all over his face. He had a point.

Despite the simplicity of this theory, another thought was stirring in my head. During my biology lectures I became fascinated with a new area of biology referred to as genetics and particularly the evolution, from the first simple organic molecules, to the RNA-DNA complex. They built the first living cell and eventually all of us. It was clear to me that DNA would have a big role to play in how we lived our lives and survived.

Suddenly there was a shrill scream. Steve and I sat along a laboratory bench at the back of the room. In front of us lay another bench with three girls also taking part in the practical. The scream came from the girl immediately in front of me who was in the midst of her dissection. She had been given an exceptionally beautiful white rabbit. Attempting to cut away the muscle tissue, the rabbit had revived and was attempting to pull itself free of the skewers stuck through its paws. The girl stared at this horrific scene and then fainted. Everyone rushed to help her and the rabbit was taken away. The girl, however recovered quickly enabling the rest of us, even if a little stunned and bewildered to continue the practical.

Lunchtime came as a welcome break. We left the laboratory, and were walking silently along a long corridor. I could see a young girl walking towards us. She had short cropped fair hair and was wearing a suede maroon midi-skirt and white blouse. She had large brown eyes which I suddenly noticed were staring right at me. I glanced away then looked straight back immediately to see that she was not only still staring but also smiling at me. What a thrill. It seemed that no one else had noticed. She passed by and I surreptitiously turned to watch her. I watched her reach the end of the corridor when she suddenly turned and stared right at me again. I was embarrassed and excited at the same time and rapidly turning to jelly.

"She looks just right for you," suggested Steve as we entered the canteen. I tried to compose myself.

"Do you know who she is?"

"No idea," said Steve emphatically.

We steered our way to the serving hatch, the thoughts of this young lady still bubbling in my mind. Meanwhile it was a choice of leathery egg or dried, hard baked chili con carne. I chose the egg together with the ubiquitous supply of baked beans. Peter and Steve sat together at the end of the table. As I sat next to them and began to forage into the doubtful feast, I found myself looking around the hall. Although it was a refectory, it doubled as a dancehall at weekends and because it was so large, for some it was also a place to study. It had a high ceiling and the sound of voices tended to merge into a general hum. Today, however, it was relatively empty. Sebastian Cox, a charismatic figure in the university, was holding forth on an adjacent table. Two of his disciples listened intently as he gestured authoritatively. He was a master of the spoken language, smooth and dangerous but fascinating. Able to reduce his fellow students to whimpering fools by his cool, ruthless and manipulative oratory. Strangely it was just the type that was likely to suffer most that was drawn into his counselling. If Charles Manson had a brother, it was Sebastian. Briefly his gaze was directed towards our table. I felt threatened and immediately looked back to the relative safety of our own table.

By now, Peter and Steve were beginning to cook up a storm as a parade of girls from the hockey team walked by, complete with short hockey skirts. Then one of them accidentally dropped a sixpence on the floor as she searched for change. She immediately bent down to retrieve it.

"Wow," exclaimed Peter.

The view was there for everyone to see. Scores from one to ten were being liberally assigned. Not all of this attention was being appreciated by some of the girls of course, one of who turned and glared menacingly at Peter. Undeterred a loud 7.5 rang out from Peter.

"That's a bit high isn't it after the stare she gave you," Steve was puzzled.

"Anybody got a sixpence?" shrieked Peter, wanting to continue the exercise.

CHAPTER TWO

Besides the never-ending succession of lectures and the inspired, and not so inspired debates, College life also provided a wealth of opportunity to meet the opposite sex and develop relationships. In my case this potential was enhanced by the fact that Bedford College had been a few years earlier for ladies only and was now sporting a ratio of 60:40 in favour of the male. Despite this unparalleled start I had not yet succeeded in finding a girlfriend. Even the girl with the big brown eyes had not reappeared.

Of course, many of the girls seemed unbelievingly attractive. The hormones, at this age, were firmly established and doing their work. At times it felt uncontrollable. I'd have to calm myself. I would try sobering thoughts such as the potential threat of religious chastisement, physical deformity, famine, the plague....anything! It never worked. The very next girl that walked by started up the whole process again. Without doubt girls were irresistible.

One such girl I met at a college "Hop." She was called Jane. Blonde and shapely and in the very low light of the dance floor quite attractive. I remember it well. The Hop was held in the college sitting room area but was not well attended. I had wandered in without having to pay and began to survey the scene. Jane stood with her back to the bar on the other side of the room and I noticed her watch me as I made my way over to get a drink.

"Before you do that would you like to dance?" she said without introduction.

Of course, I wasn't surprised at this. After all I secretly held an innate belief that all girls found me irresistible, despite what the mirror might say. It was only now, finally, after 18 years of them somehow managing to keep their distance, that one of them had finally succumbed.

We danced. I felt clumsy and tried to moderate my dance movements. She seemed to sense my hesitation and pulled me closer to her. She was warm and friendly and it felt good. Much better than I'd expected. As we talked a little it became obvious from her accent that she came from the south of England. Her manner was confident and reassured. This was my first close encounter with a lady from the south, a thought that suddenly made me acutely aware of my own northern extraction.

Despite my misplaced confidence I instinctively knew this situation was doomed. There was no way a cultured accent like hers was going to be interested in me. Maybe one dance perhaps but then definitely on her way. Yet despite these reservations she did warm to me. We seemed to enjoy the same sense of fun which I tried my best to provide. It was effortless. Nevertheless, the fear of impending silence loomed uppermost in my mind and I felt uncomfortable. After all, without a sense of fun what was there, for she seemed a very distinguished lady.

"Would you like to come to a party tomorrow night? Some friends of mine are coming from home, but I still would like you to come."

"I presume you mean your boyfriend when you say friends from home?" I suddenly had visions of having to be terribly adult and sophisticated.

"Oh darling you do make me smile" she said conspicuously. The phrase rang out.

"Oh darling!!" I repeated to myself. I was just not used to this type of vocabulary.

The mere sound of it grated in my ear and jangled loudly. My illusions were being shattered. Despite this I was not going to let it go that easy. Somehow, I put the pieces back together and tried to ignore it. She continued and explained the friends did include a boy she was quite friendly with but that she still would very much like it if I came. I accepted. It never occurred to me to say no.

The party was the following night, held at a large but dilapidated flat near Queens Park underground station. Before I reached it, the house could already be distinguished by the dull red and green haze of lights at the windows and the throb of "Money" by the now, ever present, Beatles. I arrived by myself, full of expectancy. Any party was a rare event and this one had the promise of excitement. The vibrant music pierced every part of your body as you entered. The atmosphere was loud with anticipation. People were everywhere, huddled close in intimate conversation. Their posture suggested an urgency and intensity in what they had to say. It was a warm evening which seemed to add to the ambience. The dress was down market casual, wall to wall jeans. No one seemed to know or mind if I had been invited as I made my way down the hall towards the kitchen where I could see the drinks. I was wearing a short white boiler suit jacket, high fashion at the time. No need to deposit the coat, I'd probably never see it again, just head straight for the refreshments. The kitchen was littered with beer cans, wine bottles and some rather dubious looking French bread. With a drink in my hand I set off to investigate.

The house was an endless labyrinth of rooms and stairways. I eased my way passed, what seemed like a sea of strangers, recognising no one until I glimpsed Jane as I reached the third floor.

"My goodness," taken a little by surprise, "she is attractive."

Two smooth cut guys engaged her in conversation. I stood nearby to listen and observe. The controlled nature of their conversation was impressive. As I drew closer, I could feel any attempt by me to speak was going to be an embarrassment. And so it was. Just couldn't stop myself. My initial words sounded childlike and ineffectual in comparison. Jane acknowledged me with a smile and proceeded to introduce me to her friends. So, these were the friends. I remember thinking they looked quite different to the others at the party. They wore suits and had a hairstyle to match. They were clearly representative of the Stockbroker Belt, I decided. Not that I really understood what a stockbroker really was in those days.

After the introductions their discussions continued with the same authority and calm. The tone and syntax were totally alien to me. I'd only ever heard this kind of prose on the BBC before. I stood there like a wall flower for a few minutes until a break in their conversation allowed Jane to lead me away to another part of the room. I hated the feeling of being led. We began to talk and giggle. She was happy to do that and so was I.

Now I'd not been to such a large gathering as this before and as time passed it slowly began to dawn on me that the party would go on all night and that Jane wanted me to stay. Easier said than done. The problem was that I had made no arrangements with the landlady and she was certainly a force to be reckoned with. It didn't take too much imagination to envisage the abuse I would receive the following day. It was, however, a fleeting thought which counted for nothing as the time began to march on.

By now some people were beginning to leave and others sat down around the edges of the room leaving Jane and I dancing in slow smooch style.

"Girls like you don't go out with guys like me," I ventured at one stage.

"What sort of girl does that make me?" replied Jane in mock indignation.

"I don't know, what sort of girl are you?"

She thought a little before replying. "Well I'm not a virgin, that's for sure."

There was a silence whilst I thought about that. I never expected her to say such a thing. Before I could answer she turned towards the edge of the room and we sat down. She moved close and began to cuddle. Her response was warm and inviting. My experience in such situations had never extended any further than this before and I was becoming increasingly conscience of events possibly proceeding further.

"Which one of those guys was your boyfriend," I asked bluntly.

"Neither," she said calmly, "He wasn't here. I didn't tell him about it."

I was a little surprised by this. I thought all of this was to be a show of southern sophistication.

"So, will he get to know about this?"

"I don't know," she said again with hesitation, "I'm just pausing for thought, you might say."

Without another word Jane stood up and beckoned me into an adjacent room. It was a bedroom. Piles of coats had been strewn on the floor. In the murky light of the room I could make out there were two couples in bed already. There was a third bed. We got into it fully clothed and cuddled a little more, but for some strange reason I couldn't develop this any further. There I was, fully dressed and hesitating. We lay like this a long time. Despite everything we were still relative strangers. In fact, I still didn't know her full name. But why was I thinking and not doing. This was an opportunity, the very first opportunity to do something my hormones had been thinking desperately about for years. The physical attraction was beyond dispute. The thinking continued until I eventually fell asleep. And that was that.

In the cold light of the following day I felt uncomfortable and embarrassed. The smell in the room was now distinctly acrid and as I looked around everything seemed ugly and depressive. Even Jane didn't look so pretty anymore and to my horror she sat up and removed her hair! It was a wig. The shock of this discovery depressed me even further. After a few awkward words I left and made my way through the debris out into the morning air. It seemed clean, pure and refreshing, but inwardly I felt wretched and glad to have escaped.

To be out at this time in the early morning seemed odd and added to the growing discomfort I was feeling about the situation. A feeling which began to take on new dimensions when I thought of returning to my digs. It was 4.00 am and still dark. Although the house was potentially large enough to sneak in without notice, it still required someone to unbolt the door on the inside.

Finally, the house stood before me, its dark foreboding shape silhouetted against the moonlit sky like a gothic tombstone. A clear picture of an irate Mrs. Carter stood, complete with pitchfork and other suitable instruments of torture, played with tantalising realism as I imagined her opening the door.

My bedroom was at the front of the house, so on arrival, I tried throwing a few very small pebbles tentatively at the window with the vain hope of waking somebody other than Mrs. Carter. I waited a long time. Then suddenly I heard a faint noise at the door. Slowly it edged open. I really didn't know what to expect. I almost decided to turn and make a run for it, when a disheveled looking Andy peered disgruntedly from around the door. What a relief. He turned without further acknowledgement, and immediately stalked silently back up the stairs. I followed rather sheepishly behind. Mission accomplished, but not without damage. But I did manage a couple of hours sleep.

Now breakfast at Mrs. Carters was a tense affair. Everyone should be at their appointed place at the breakfast table at the appointed time. After breakfast was served, nothing was to be left on the plate. She accepted no help. The food was dutifully brought in monastic silence.

That morning, as might be expected, was begun with Andy scornfully relating the early mornings escapades.

"I presume you all heard the fuss this morning?" said Andy as an opening gambit.

"Were you locked out Nicholas?" followed Aaron sarcastically. He always used the full name when he intended to be sarcastic.

"I won't ask her name," Gary's tone was more friendly, "Was it a good party?"

Before I could answer Andy interrupted, "Which one was it?" he asked demandingly, "I saw Amy yesterday, she was asking after you."

To mention this person nicely exaggerated the situation. Particularly since I couldn't really bring any Amy to mind. I was beginning to feel distinctly exposed and a distaste for the whole night's episode was returning fast. Brian continued the theme with a spontaneous rendering of Georgie Porgie kissed the girls and made them cry followed by Aaron repeating,

"Or in Nick's case, Georgie Porgie kissed the girls and….pulled their knickers down"

They all laughed.

Such was the morning. The morning also included a 9.00am lecture. Miraculously I arrived awake but sore and hesitantly took my place. The lecture room was reminiscent of a small classroom complete with small and well used traditional desks. My head was filled with a drone from not enough sleep. The room seemed dark, and filled with muffled echoey noises as the other students shuffled in. In front of me sat Lauren and Francis. I noticed them straight away because I was still feeling awkward about previous events. In my imagination, they represented Miss Prim and Miss Proper. They appeared so correct and dignified. They generally remained aloof from little boys like me, or so it seemed. Relief came as Dr. Banham, the lecturer and a very amiable person, began his account of Pleistocene geology. His presentation technique was so well rehearsed and confident that the voice began to exaggerate inflexions on certain words as he paced up down the front of the room.

"And so, it began…….and the world rejoiced as the seas

retreated.......but such was the power of the glaciers..." he would occasionally bellow with emotion.

It was as though he was in a religious fervor or acting the role of Olivier reciting some monologue from Hamlet. I found it amusing and always wished he would develop it further. But eventually he would compose himself and be content to leave it. I took notes, trying hard to keep some order and neatness about them. I would never return to them again until exam time.

At the end of the lecture was a short break before the next at 10.30am, time enough for a coffee and a chance to develop relationships. Today, however, I wanted none of that. I needed a friendly face and so I went to find Gary. I found him in an enthusiastic mood. After leaving college he always insisted that he had a very earnest intention to go into research. This morning, however, he had a quite different idea. He wanted to buy a double decker bus, paint it decoratively, drive it to the south of France and sell fish and chips to the tourists. We mused over the possibilities.

As the day proceeded and the evening approached my head began to clear. I had nothing special arranged and so made my way to one of the large halls. Each of the halls had a piano. I would always steal as much time as possible to play. I was not a gifted piano player, no such luck, and everything I played was by "ear". It was a limited style, but I needed to play. To discover a new chord sequence, a new syncopation, was thrilling. Nearly all the music I played was original but only in the sense that I didn't know how to play other people's tunes. So, each time I played depended very much on how I felt that day. It would be a voyage of discovery, feeling for new or interesting sounds and themes whilst holding to established safe and harmonious areas. This may sound a little grandiose but it's not intended. I didn't care if I was bad or good, I needed to play like I needed food. It was just great therapy and it allowed me to weave day to day emotions into a tapestry of sound, almost as if entering thoughts into a diary.

It was my music which took me to Tin Pan Alley, Soho in search of an agent which would willing to produce my songs. I selected 3 songs which I had previously recorded on my basic tape recorder.

The first few agents were not interested. Some of them didn't even have a tape recorder and so asked me to play on their piano but to no avail. A second visit was more successful. A music publisher called Brian Webb liked the recordings and arranged for me to re-record them at a private studio close by.

I practiced as much as possible for a week before the big day. It was a very exciting event for me and I was very nervous as I entered a rather run down room. Nevertheless, appearances mattered not. Cables, microphones and amplifiers were everywhere. To my surprise there was even a bass player and a drummer waiting, and ready to go. Having never seen them before I became worried. I looked at Brian.

"Do they know my songs?"
"Oh yes, no problem," he said confidently. "Shall we make a start?" nodding to the bass player.

"Are we not having practice run first," I said, anxiously.

"I don't think we need it." Again Brian looked at the bass player and he nodded.

Brian looked at me wanting me to sit down at an upright

piano. I played a few notes of the first song 'If You Really Don't know'

"Ok that's fine," He then looked over to a raised window which I hadn't noticed before. A guy appeared at the window giving a thumbs up. Presumably, my few notes were a sound check! Everything was moving so fast….too fast. The drummer began the introduction when I suddenly realised I had to begin. I managed to complete the song.

Brian looked up at the window and got a thumbs up.
"Ok that's a take," he announced. "Next song, Somebody's Talking".

"Brian! I thought 'If you really don't know' was too fast. Can we do it again?"

"No, that was fine, no mistakes," he replied authoratively.

The next song went the same way. Far too fast and lacked syncopation. Finally, it was time for the third and last song "Witchatana". It was a ballad and I started this one on the piano. It went well with a nice moody beat.
"That was great," said Brian. "Three songs completed in three tracks. How about that boys!" They nodded in agreement.

"They were three excellent songs," remarked the bass player. He seemed genuinely impressed.

Suddenly I remembered I had a lecture coming up in half an hour. There was no time to enjoy the moment. Fortunately, I made it to the lecture, my head still buzzing with the music and as soon as the lecture finished, I was off to find a piano, hopefully in Tuke's Hall. I approached the hall through one of the many dark creaking, wooden, floored corridors to the rear and entered through a door that revealed a maze of tall, towering drapes which formed the backdrop of the stage. They hung like giant flags and began to billow and wave as I searched my way through to the main part of the stage.

"Let's try again," said a muffled voice in the distance, "I think the choristers could sing a little softer as they approach the last verse."

I stopped in my tracks. The hall was occupied. This would mean I wouldn't be able to play this evening. I immediately felt a mild discomfort like withdrawal symptoms. The Gilbert & Sullivan Society were rehearsing their next performance. I sneaked quietly back out and decided to make my way to the auditorium to watch. Dr. Bridgstone and Dr. Bishop were the principal supporters of this group. They were both lecturers in Geology and tremendously enthusiastic about light opera. It was a dress rehearsal. All the faces were made up and looked pale and anemic. The lips were painted bright red in contrast and their hair tied back revealing the full harshness of their features. Why anyone would want to appear in public looking like that, I could never understand. The atmosphere was organised. A sense of activity always appeared to be an important constituent of any member. Conversations consisted almost entirely of instruction and orders and there was not enough genuine communication for my liking. Lauren and Francis, however, appeared to revel in the proceedings, their voices at times audible above all others.

The time was now almost 6.30 pm, and time to eat. So, feeling restless, I got up and made my way down to the canteen. At this time, it was sparsely occupied. I paid my one and sixpence and headed towards a space at the end of one of the tables. The egg seemed dry and over cooked, but it tasted ok. I made a reconnoiter of the hall. Only a few solitary figures. They sat alone, some with books others just dozing, slouched awkwardly in their chairs. Closer by, at the end of my row of tables was Sebastian Cox again and his two disciples in more playful mood. Always fascinated I tried to eaves drop on their conversation. It wasn't to be. Suddenly the hush in the hall was broken.

"Why is this guy sitting all on his own, then?" said an almost shrill, but comic, voice from behind. "He looks so bored!"

I recognised the voice. It was Peter together with James.

"Well we're going to change all that, aren't we, 'cos we're going to sit here as well," said Peter continuing the performance.

"Yep, it's too late now cos we're here now," followed James in an equally animated tone.

Oliver, another student geologist also joined them as they deliberately continued the fuss of sitting down. I caught a glimpse of Sebastian as he turned his head away in semi-disdain at the intrusion of this noise. It mattered not, I was very pleased to see them. Their humor was instant and fun, even if at times mockingly infantile.

"There's no need to sulk you know," began Peter again, "Is there Oliver?"

"No need to sulk at all," confirmed Oliver.

"Why doesn't he need to sulk?" interceded James as he stared at the unusual color of the minced meat in his shepherd's pie. This type of nonsense conversation was just a form of greeting for Peter. He continued.

"Well I've just seen Doctor B," using his affectionate name for Dr. Bridgstone, "and she says the Cheese and Wine Seminar is tomorrow and not to forget....and be sure to tell that Nick not to sulk."

"Why should I sulk, Peter, when there are guys like you around" I weakly retorted finally able to find space.

Peter feigned offence. "Words Nicholas, they're merely words," and then without pause, "incidentally I have one word for you."

"And that is?"

"Fred Hoyle," clearly using two words, but I wasn't about to rise to that. "I went to hear him talk at UC yesterday evening and he's got something. He talks about the cosmos, space travel and everything. But it's the way he ties these things together"

"With a name like that he doesn't sound very cosmic," I said unbelievingly.

"Cosmic, man," said James flatly as he watched a brightly yellow colored stain of custard run down the front of his bright red jumper.

"It was all about the origin of life, and it began, not here on earth, but out there in the galaxy somewhere, millions of years before it arrived here on earth," said Peter emphatically.

James continued to stare down at the changing pattern on his jumper as he vacantly debated whether to lick the custard off directly.

"Amen," Oliver was not impressed.

"The basic molecules required for the construction of organic matter have been found in meteorites. They are rich in organic chemicals".

Peter's eyes seem to glow as he gazed upwards towards an imaginary meteorite. He continued to hold our attention despite the urgent attention required to James' jumper.

I liked what he said.

"Thus, the origin of organic molecules, the building blocks for life were already prefabricated in other parts of the galaxy,"

"How convenient," said James, with a faint edge of sarcasm.

"It could even be that the some of these molecules had evolved further, even as far as DNA and the first cell!" exclaimed Peter.

"Even more convenient," added Oliver, echoing James' previous hint of sarcasm.

It looked like Peter was not going to continue.

"What is it with you two? This is interesting.......Isn't it?" I was becoming very aware of their growing boredom. Both James and Oliver shook their heads emphatically. They were ready to move on. To make their point they both stood up noisily and pointed in the general direction of the bar. Sebastian Cox turned and scornfully scrutinised why the peace of the refectory had been shattered yet again. As we walked along the corridor Peter finished off his story.

Certainly, the visit of Peter to the lecture at UC was very timely. It seemed to clarify so much about the beginnings of life. I was convinced that all our behavior, even our most reverent of thoughts or emotions was only physics in action. A simple equation of mass and energy being forced to establish a correct balance and then trying to sustain it. In fact, it was the way that particles, atoms and molecules behaved that interested me. They brought together their constituents brutally, grabbing particles at will.

"Isn't that process selfish?" mumbling to myself. "That surely could be considered selfish behavior? That's the physics controlling our behavior. So, maybe it's possible to consider it is this process of selfish behavior that secures the survival of the entire Universe and life itself."

I passed some of these thoughts onto Peter who immediately added that behavior was simply a prelude to sex. He intended this as a joke, but somehow it also had a ring of truth about it. In fact, this last comment attracted the interest of James.

"What do you think of my behavior Peter?" raising an arm and conspicuously scratching his armpit.

"It's abysmal," came the immediate response.

"Does that mean you won't have sex with me?" said James indignantly.

"That's right," replied Peter without expression.

"Really, you won't?" said James yet again.

"Nope, I'm sorry but I will not have sex with you." Peter's voice had taken on a fatherly tone.

"If I promise to behave myself?" came the enquiry again.

"Well you'd have to improve a lot," said Peter, appearing to yield a little.

"Then will you take me to the dance?" pointing to a poster on the corridor wall. "Please, please!"

They proceeded down the corridor with the continuing sound of this most eccentric of conversations. Oliver and I stared at each other with a bemused look.

"Talking of which, are you going to the dance at Hanover Lodge?"

Oliver looked shocked. "I hope you're not asking me to take you," taking a step back.

"I'll take that as a no, then."

Oliver had classical good looks and was quite attached to a girl with equally good classical looks. However, it was always curious that whenever quizzed about the young ladies in his life, present or past, he never succumbed to details. Perhaps this was an air of mystery he liked to cultivate about himself. On the other hand, it left me with the feeling he was up to something.

The corridor was quite dark now, almost without windows, lit only by the light emanating from the lounge ahead of us. The walls were used to pin notices of the forthcoming social and society events.

"Hey, look its Julie Driscoll on at the dance," I said in surprise.

"Can't be bad," he added with satisfaction.

As we entered the lounge and then the bar, I suddenly spotted Jane. She was sitting with two male students whom I had vaguely seen talking to her before. To me they looked like another world. It did not seem natural to step outside of this zany group of companions but, somehow I felt obliged to go over and say hello. I weakly excused myself. Their sudden silence, as I crossed this void, made me feel even more self-conscious.

The two students wore earthy, military like, jackets which were fast becoming fashionable items to the so-called elite of the socially aware. They looked at my simple brown jumper in judgement and waited for me to say something. Jane, however, was still talking quite earnestly it seemed about a relationship. I didn't know whose. She saw me and stopped.

"Nick!" she said with almost forced enthusiasm. "There's a party and I want you to come." By the time she had reached the end of the sentence she almost sounded convincing. "Bring your guitar," Before I could stop myself, I had said yes. I just couldn't think of an excuse fast enough. Inwardly I grimaced. I looked over to Peter, aware that they may be watching, but fortunately they were looking in the other direction.

"No immediate rescue there," I thought.

Jane stood up and grabbed my arm.

"Come on, I'll drive you to Swiss Cottage with me so I can get changed." She spoke with genuine enthusiasm. This sounded better and immediately I began to relax. From a cold start the situation was beginning to improve. She continued to hold onto my arm as we left and now suddenly, the feeling was warm and inviting. In any case she had a new mini, a major attraction in those days.

The thought of another party so soon seemed a little odd to me, but such were the times and Jane was insistent. We reached Swiss Cottage and Dorchester Place, an "all girl's" hall of residence. We went upstairs to her room. She changed in front of me revealing without affectation her almost naked body. I was spellbound by this display. Surprised, I was uncertain how to react. My inexperience in these matters was really beginning to show. In fact, I had never had any "physical" relationship with a female. Especially an attractive female. There was no uncertainty of how my body had now, without my personal permission, transformed into a pulsating, lust full, wobbling jelly. Somehow at this stage, my naivety thought it might be impolite to reveal the full uncontrollable extent of this. I pretended, the best I could, to be unimpressed; as though I was overly familiar with such situations. Perhaps too well. I sat there locked in space, motionless unable for some unfathomable reason to pursue a more lustful course as she brushed passed me, leaning this way and that as she searched out her underwear. Everything seemed to be happening so quickly. At the same time, I suddenly noticed the wig sitting perched like an insect on the dressing table. I could have sworn it turned and winked at me. I looked elsewhere in the room for a distraction.

It was a narrow room with a high ceiling and a polished but rickety wooden floor. Many pairs of discarded shoes were loosely assembled around the edges of a central carpet. The dark furniture was old and well used but each, no doubt, with its own, particular history. The room was not untidy, but it was decoratively ornamented with the occasional item of clothing. Before today the female world had always been a closed door. Proximity of this kind I had not previously experienced. Except for the insect like wig, it felt good.

The show over, she sat at the dressing table to brush her hair, her real hair. I leaned over to give her a kiss. It seemed awkward as though I didn't really know her well enough. Yet it seemed perfectly in order, for her to take her clothes off in front of me. Whatever the reason I'd missed the moment. I had a lot to learn. Be that as it may, it was now party time.

"Do you want to drive" she asked.

"Not particularly," I said, "It's ok if you want to." London traffic and a strange car didn't really appeal at that moment.

"Only some fellas hate to be driven."

"No, you can do the work whilst I sort out my masculinity problems," I replied sitting back in my seat to make myself comfortable.

"Have you got some sort of problem then?" She was clearly referring to my lack of activity.

"I don't actually know yet." I mused to my virginal self.

The thought suddenly crossed my mind "What if I did?" At this stage I couldn't really pinpoint the reason for my self-control. There was no lack of physical desire. It had crossed my mind that she might have some sort of gruesome sexually transmittable disease. I hadn't even began to think about condoms. The thought of starting such a discussion seemed to turn me off the whole idea. I suddenly realised that this whole business was not as simple as it seemed.

"You don't look as though you've got a problem, although I wish you wouldn't tell me so many jokes"

"Whoops....She doesn't like the jokes." My heart sank. I was under the impression that she liked the jokes. "Now I do have a problem." I felt very foolish. Not surprisingly the remaining car journey was silent. We were on our way to my digs to pick up my guitar. There was no joy in my heart and if Aaron sees me now, he can only add to the frustration. He wasn't there and the house was cold and empty and suddenly the thoughts of a party didn't seem so bad even with a bruised ego.

We drove on to arrive at yet another dilapidated flat. I turned to Jane and for some incomprehensible reason, I ventured, a completely different approach. "Have you ever thought that everything we do is selfish?" She stared at me in astonishment and appeared distinctly irritated.

"Have I what??" she uttered disdainfully, her attention clearly elsewhere.

"Have you ever......," I began but then stopped. I finally came to my senses. What was I thinking!

The spontaneity I had with Jane previously, of course, had all but disappeared. During the party she talked more with her friends. Being left alone I was more aware of the poor state of the place. Everywhere layers of dust were conspicuous. Only where surfaces had been used for bottles or glasses had the dust retreated. Spilt drinks had mingled and created small dust filled beads and rivulets of beer or wine. I edged myself away from the walls and tried not to lean on anything. In another room I could see people smoking in a conspicuous and slightly exaggerated manner. The aroma was distinctive. I suddenly became aware of my brown jumper again.

Jane came over to me. "I want to go now, will you come with me?"

I was surprised at the softness of her tone. She took my hand and then affectionately gave me a hug. I didn't really understand this change. She looked up at me.

"You didn't play your guitar."

"It's not really a guitar." I began. "It's more like a harp."

"And no one asked you to play it," followed Jane.

"But then we shouldn't joke, should we," I added tentatively. She smiled.

"Let's go if we're going," I continued with purpose in my voice. I was beginning to get a better feeling inside.

We arrived back at the Hall in Swiss Cottage. As I stood outside the car Jane closed her door, paused, and then leaned against the car.

"Nick," she began. "I do have another boyfriend. One of those chaps I was talking to this evening." I listened. "I've known him a long time." I waited for her to finish.

"He's actually my fiancé," she said hesitantly. "And we get married in September."

For a moment I froze. I've never been interested in jewelry before but now I found myself looking intently at her fingers. Sure enough, there was the ring. Whether it had just appeared I couldn't really say since I'd never looked before.

"So why this?" trying not to look hurt. A noise began to buzz in my head.

"Why did you want to........." I was starting to fluster.

"You're nice and I liked you." The words sounded warm and friendly, but I was in pain.

"I think it's that way to West Hampstead," I said in the same uncertain voice. I picked up my guitar and began to walk.

"Will you get back alright?" I raised my arm in the air but didn't look back.

The walk home was tinged with regret but also relief. At least the rain had stopped and it was warm. I remember thinking why on earth I had put myself through this. From the moment we had met my instincts told me something was wrong. Even that this was likely to happen.

It was 2.30am as I stood outside my digs staring up at the moonlit sky. The house was in total darkness and here I was again "locked out." A slight breeze rustled the leaves in the trees lining the street. This time I decided to try Gary's window and give Andy a miss. "What a mess" I thought. After the night I'd just had this was just getting more silly. I walked down the narrow passage to the side of the house. I'd never seen the rear of the house before and for the first time realized it backed onto a railway cutting. The low rumble of a train could just be heard as it passed by, deep in the cutting. Armed with a few small pebbles I threw them delicately at Gary's window. At that same instant I suddenly realised it could just as easily have been Mrs. Carters room. I quickly did a recheck of the house layout in my mind. It wasn't that easy to be sure with these large rambling Edwardian houses. I breathed a sigh of relief as Gary appeared at the window. He still looked asleep as he opened the door to let me in. He turned around immediately to go back upstairs. I followed. I went to the bathroom to wash away the taste of the evening. As quietly as possible I tried to turn on the cold water tap without disturbing anybody. Suddenly a voice whispered, "Are you ok?" It was Gary. As I lifted my head to speak, I hit the narrow shelf above the sink which had a single glass on it. The glass fell with a crash into the sink. Besides the noise there was sure to be glass everywhere. To my surprise the glass hadn't broken. Incredulously, however, the large porcelain sink had cracked and split visibly into two halves. The stupid glass was still in one piece. Gary stared disbelievingly at the newly sculptured sink.

"How are you going to tell Mrs. Carter," whispered Gary anxiously. "She'll kill you when she finds out." His tone was frightened as though it was going to happen to him. I finally spoke.

"Shit," and then again "Shit." After staring at it for what seemed an eternity. I then mumbled, "And that glass is still in one piece." I reluctantly resigned myself to the worst. "I'll just have to tell her in the morning," I whispered as Gary turned to go. I just longed for this night to end.

The night did end, but the morning began again, in exactly the same way. I was late getting up and Mrs. Carter was waiting for me in the hallway. Aaron was lurking behind her waiting for me with his usual gaunt expression which he delighted in turning into an exaggerated cheesy grin. She already knew about the basin and after some fairly obvious statements, some quite personal, I was visibly beginning to ebb. I went through to the breakfast room. Everyone was there. There was silence as they watched me take my place at the table. No one spoke. The cheesy grin on Aaron's face, however, was now virtually out of control. His arms were held straight and tight down the side of him as he manically gripped the base of his chair. Such was his enthusiasm to begin. He rocked slightly as his head turned animatedly from side to side waiting impatiently. Finally, he could wait no longer.

"Well," he began, lingering on the word. "What a performance." He looked again to the others to join in. "What do you think Andy?" trying again. "Would you go in for this sort of thing?" Andy began with a smile and then a half smirk and then finally almost laughing he said, "It's certainly unusual, isn't it, Aaron?" They could see me wilting. Aaron began again.

"Do you think it's carelessness or just stupidity," he suggested for general consideration. Then with a mocking laugh he shrieked, "She will definitely throw you out!" He was enjoying this so much he almost choked on a piece of bacon. I just had to say something.

"Aaron I'm glad this is providing you with some sort of entertainment, and that you can see the funny side. In fact, if you carry on much longer you will have a convulsion which would please me a lot, but it wouldn't be a pretty sight. What ever happened is none of your business so just cut the crap and get on with your breakfast," I said trying remain calm. In reality I wanted to strangle him.

"Oh....Oh..." he continued. "Swearing now is it. I wonder what Mrs. Carter would say if she heard that.

In came Mrs. Carter and Aaron was silenced. She served out the eggs and bacon and as quickly as she came in, she disappeared. Gary tried a few rallying remarks on my behalf, but Aaron was unstoppable.

It was to be a long day. A lot of it spent avoiding any further contact with Aaron or Andy or even Jane. One person I couldn't avoid was Peter. His manner was quite nonchalant as made his way along the corridor. Even at this distance I could see the ever-present twinkle in his eye as they almost bulged from within those thick lenses he had. Despite the day I had had, I suspected all wasn't well within his recent engagement to Susan. He was very private about this area, at least he was with me. Whenever I was in his company and there arose the possibility to ask such types of questions I always decided otherwise at the last second. It seemed somehow, imprudent to follow through. There were somedays that the moments between his almost continuous flow of zaniness were filled with a concern, even anguish. It worried me right there and then just to think about it. But all of this was surmise on my part and I could be way off the mark.

Peter stopped and stood very close, in front of me, just inside my area of personal space. He did this deliberately of course just to provoke a reaction. I called his bluff and did not move or speak. There was an agonising moment as the closeness became almost unbearable. Peter yielded.

"Did you lose some money?" he asked, as he stepped clumsily backwards. I breathed a sigh of relief to have my space back and then looked at him curiously.

"You look so glum." He was right, I did.

"I'm recuperating." I replied. Now, whenever I see Peter of late, I've tended to hit him with the same old subject, that is, the meaning of life and girls. The conversation, on these particular topics ran the risk, therefore, of becoming a forbidden item if I wasn't careful. I had, however, been making some progress and really wanted to test the latest theory out and he was the only one so far who maintained any semblance of interest. I chanced it with a bold statement.

"I've been thinking about how the brain works"

"Whose brain are we talking about?" he said wryly. I decided to try and skip the small talk and press on, but then changed my mind.

"You've been dumped. Haven't you?" he said pointedly.

"Thanks, how did you know?"

"Why? What went wrong?" he immediately responded.

"I don't know...well I do....well I think I do."
I tried hard not to be emotional about it.

"I knew she would," spoken with an element of satisfaction.

"I'm not happy about it….." I paused "No….Actually I am happy about it," I said more cheerily. "We were not really suited and I couldn't pretend anymore and neither could she."

"Well if that's how you were feeling, it's no wonder you were dumped," said Peter, "Hey!" he shrieked suddenly, "Our lecture, it's started!"

We entered the corridor and dived into the next lecture room. It was the last lecture of the day. Afterwards, Peter made his excuses and disappeared. It seemed everyone else had also disappeared without trace and I was left alone with my thoughts. It had been a long night and a long day. Outside, the evening was drawing in. I leaned against the window to see the last little bit of the sunshine before the blackness of the night terminated the day. Two people ran across the lawn and then stopped briefly in front of the window. They cuddled affectionately. It was Jane and her fiancé. I turned away. I felt my body grow tense as all the confusion of the day returned. The tension made me walk forcefully along the corridor. I walked along another corridor and then another. I didn't want to stop until this feeling went away.

Luckily, some help was on hand. I found myself outside Tuke Hall. If it was free, I could play the piano. That would be all the therapy I needed. And it was. That evening I played a symphony. It was to all that girls could be and all they were not; to the worst in life and to the best. No one heard it but me, but I felt great again.

CHAPTER THREE

The next day I hurriedly bought a few notebooks and note pads before attending the first lectures. The words went in as neatly as possible. With new notebooks I always began with good intentions of keeping a full and comprehensive set of lecture notes. The subject was interesting and at times entertaining and at these moments I would chastise myself for not taking time to read in depth. This time I had serious plans. I was going to make more use of the library and devote more time to follow up reading. But then I wondered if I really would. I hadn't been too successful so far. University was my first taste of freedom and although I didn't realise it at the time, I was wasting a tremendous amount of time with music and social affairs rather than applying myself. Time seemed to be in abundance. No responsibilities. No commitments. Just freedom. I thought it would go on forever.

As I finished the last lecture of the day, Steve Donaldson approached. He was a geology acquaintance whom I'd got to know a little playing football in the college 1st XI.

"All set for the first match on Sunday?" he asked in a friendly tone.

"Is the team up on the board then?" realising it was that time of year again.

"Yep, it's at home," I looked down along the corridor towards the notice board.

"I'll go and have a look. See if my name's there." It was.

"Would you like to come with Oliver and myself to see Chelsea play Tottenham tonight?" The offer sounded tempting. I'd never seen a 1st Division match before, so this seemed like an excellent idea. I agreed enthusiastically, realising that my good intentions to visit the library were being postponed yet again.

We made our arrangements and deciding there was enough time to snatch a bite to eat moved off quickly towards the refectory. As I walked along the corridor a young pretty girl approached. She looked familiar. We looked at each other briefly. She smiled. I turned to look at her as she passed by. It was the same girl with the large brown eyes I had seen before. She was gorgeous.

"Come on Nick!" shouted an intruding voice. "Come on," he repeated. It was Oliver. "If we're going, we'd better get a move on."

I turned away to catch them up. We decided to skip the refectory and buy a hot dog on the way.

"Are you still going on about that science business?" asked Oliver, as we strode ever more urgently.

"I go on about it, do I?"

"Sort of. It's not exactly going on, it's just I can't see what all the fuss is about." He spoke glibly as though it really had no importance. "Your ideas and discussions seem so simple and naive…..In fact almost banal. I really can't believe that anything of this kind is so simple."

"Banal eh," I repeated, trying to keep calm. "Thanks….And you know better, do you?"

"I know there's more to heaven and earth than there is in

your philosophy, Horatio," sounding as though he was quoting from the biblical text. That was clever. But on recovering my thoughts it was also true of everything you don't understand; that is until you find out more about it.

"That seems just a defeatist attitude to me," pausing for breath. We were still walking at almost a running pace. "How can you call yourself a scientist if you don't believe in a reasonable scientific explanation?" He didn't answer. The discussion had run its course. Steve pointed towards the tube station. An abundance of blue and black scarves were now conspicuous.

The game was a local derby and attracted a large and enthusiastic crowd. As we travelled by tube and made our way towards the football ground, we found ourselves in an alleyway leading to the turnstile entrances. The growing surge of supporters engulfed us, and it wasn't long before I was unable to remove my hands from my pockets. To move my arms was impossible. I was squashed with bodies pressing in from all around. The gate entrance grew closer. I could still make out Steve and Oliver as they were being swept along ahead of me. The tide of bodies relentlessly pressed towards the gate. A sudden increase of pressure then took me by surprise. I tried to take a breath and couldn't and for a fleeting second, I felt panicked. But then relief as I was delivered into the relative safety of the turnstile entrance. It seemed to me that was a lucky escape.

It was not easy to find a place to watch and when we did it was far back from the pitch. So much so I could barely make out the players. Quite disappointing really. The atmosphere, however, was special. The roars of the crowd were loud, crackling my eardrums. Sometimes, the tension brought silence. Individual shouts of abuse rang out, taunting and jeering. It was a night to remember, Chelsea lost 0-1. Bonetti could have done better.

The weekend finally arrived and with it the Autumn Dance to be held at the Hanover Lodge. This was an all-girls hall of residence situated in the park not far away from the college. Back at the digs we all planned to go. Even Aaron was going to make an exception for this occasion. It was considered by some as the most important social event on the student calendar. Many of the girls found the whole occasion distasteful and referred to it as just a cattle market, which I suppose it was, but so it was for all of us. Nevertheless, it would be very well attended, and boy would meet girl many times during that evening. Unintentionally an anticipation was building. I could hear it in the discussions between Gary and Andy as various names were being thrown into the hat. It never occurred to me to think of asking a girl to go with me. It seemed much more interesting to arrive alone.

Finally, we were ready, clean shirts, jeans and in my case the obligatory brown jumper. No special attempt had been made to dress formally. The four of us arrived at the gates of the lodge and except for the sound of our footsteps on the fine gravel of the drive, there was little sign of activity. The lodge was a large brick, purpose-built hall of residence with regular rows of windows aligned either side of the main doorway. Their regular rectangular shapes were conspicuous only from the dull yellow glow of the distant street lighting.

We stepped into the brightly lit entrance hall. All around us we could see corridors leading out from the hallway, each of them long and straight, punctuated only by the regular, almost ominous dark rectangular shapes of the endless room doors. More people were now beginning to appear. Several girls in dressing gowns still walked to and fro, unperturbed by the visitors, only to disappear uneventfully down a corridor and into their rooms. We paused at a table to buy tickets. Ahead we could see into the darkness of the dance hall and the play of flashing green and yellow lights. Inside the hall we took our place at the far end and stared out at the still sporadically filled room. The music was subdued and at times still interrupted as the disc jockey continued to experiment with the sound. I turned towards Aaron.

"It's your turn to get the drinks," I said bravely, and to my surprise he responded.

"Alright, what do you want?" He looked reluctant. We looked at him disbelievingly and then placed our orders quickly before the moment evaporated.

"Beer."

"Beer, please."

"Beer, please Aaron."

Aaron stared sullenly around at the eager faces before him. "I think I might remember that," he said begrudgingly and then taking on a rather pained expression he turned and walked, in his characteristically stiff-backed, manner towards the bar. As we waited, more and more people continued to arrive, and within a short time, the dancing was underway. Aaron reappeared with a tray of beers in not so attractive plastic glasses. He still had a pained expression.

"What's wrong Aaron? Did it cost more than you expected?"

"No, it's not that," he said with a concerned tone "I don't really feel very well….I've only just got over having conjunctivitis." He coughed loudly making very little effort to turn his head away. Aaron was often ill or just looked ill.

It was his way. We all paused and simultaneously stared into our beers. Andy put his glass down. I cautiously took a sip of my beer and then began to study the possibilities ahead. A group of girls were stood not too far away, and I could make out the neatly cut long dark hair of one in particular, which took my attention. I prepared myself to make a bold step forward. Andy looked agitated and began to grin a toothy grin without obvious reason.

"I think Andy's going to make his move," I said jokingly, and then to my surprise he did. He strode confidently up to my dark haired girl and snatched her away. "He can't do that!" I bemoaned inwardly. But he had and I had to start again. I'm glad he did because amongst the same group of girls I recognised the same pretty face I had passed in the corridor the previous day. Without further thought, and before nerves could take over, I walked up to her and asked her to dance. There was a short silence, which under the circumstances seemed like forever. The other girls seemed to move away. The nerves were now beginning to suffer.

"Yes," she said finally. I audibly sighed with relief. We moved over to find a space on the dance floor and began to dance. She wore a maroon colored mini-length dress with a pattern of small flowers and a high collar like that of choir boys. It gave her an angelic image. Her crowning glory, however, were her brown eyes. She smiled. As we danced, I admired her well-proportioned features. I found her very attractive. I suddenly realised I was staring and so looked away. She moved closer.

"My name is Jenna," she had a friendly tone. I felt her close presence.

"Nick," introducing myself. We began to dance again.

"It's my first year…I'm studying Geography."

"You must know Aaron," I said with some irony.

"No, I don't think so," appearing a little puzzled.

"I'm in Geology…..Where are you from originally?"

"Chesterfield," she offered.

"Not far from me really…Just follow the motorway three more junctions further north." As I spoke, she was smiling. Again, I tried not to stare.

"Did you know your Spire is crooked?" trying to make a vain reference to the Parish church famous for its twisted spire. Again she looked puzzled and began to check her clothes.

"There's lots of people here…..Are you with friends?" trying to get the conversation back on track.

"With a group of girls from the Holme," The Holme was another girl's hall of residence sited close to the college, referred to as the Inner Circle.

"You make friends fast." The music came to a temporary halt. "Would you like another dance?"

"Yes, alright," she said, at least with a little enthusiasm. I was looking for any signs of encouragement.

"You're very kind," said with a smile.

"Yes, I am."

"That's good," I followed. "So am I."

"We'll see," she said poignantly. We continued dancing through two or three more records. As a result of my nervousness and the exercise I was beginning to perspire noticeably. I needed an excuse to rinse my face and cool off.

"Would you like a drink?" We stopped dancing. She picked up her leather handbag and moved towards the bar area. I was getting rather warm, so after getting a couple of drinks, I excused myself to find a wash basin. I returned to see her occupied talking to Derek, a familiar face whom I was vaguely acquainted with. He was a 2nd year Geography student. I moved into view but held back. She looked gorgeous and I wanted her, but was I too late? I remained there long enough for her to see me and to judge her reaction. What a relief, she looked pleased to see me. I went back and asked her for another dance. Derek gave me an angry look.

"Is he a boyfriend?" I asked casually. "He doesn't look very pleased."

"No, not at all. Just someone I met." I felt relieved and continued to dance. Again, I was struck by how pretty she was. However, by now we had been dancing a long time and after such a brief meeting I was anxious not to spoil things by imposing. Perhaps this was a little presumptuous of me to assume I could monopolise her entire evening. Maybe I should allow her a suitable space to escape if she so wanted. We paused for a drink and I disappeared yet again to rinse my face with some cooling water. To my surprise Derek was waiting for me in the washroom. He looked tense, trying hard to maintain an outward appearance of control.

"Are you intending to dance with Jenna all night," he said curtly.

"Ah ha…..that depends," I said cautiously.

"Well if you don't mind, I wish to dance with her."

"Did you not have your chance?" I enquired, drying my face.

"No!" he replied vehemently. I got the feeling he wasn't going to go away easily.

"Ok, I'll do this one thing. You go now and ask her to dance….I must be mad…… but there I've said it now." I couldn't believe what I had just said. Derek disappeared immediately. I slowly made my way back to the dance floor. Andy was in deep discussion with Aaron standing towards the edge of the hall. I passed them unnoticed hoping not to be delayed by what would have been unnecessary chatter. I decided enough time had now elapsed and began to speed up my return. I had an overwhelming feeling I had done a very stupid thing.
I arrived at the original spot where I had left Jenna standing on her own. They were not there. I began searching amongst the numerous faces bobbing up and down. Nothing, no signs of them. I scanned the bar area.

"Where have you been?" came a voice from behind. I turned to look. It was Jenna.

"Looking for you."

"Why did you leave me like that with Derek…..I thought we were dancing?" She spoke with a soft tone. Without hesitation I took her hand and said, "You're right. I shouldn't have left you."
We were together all evening and when it was time to go, I asked her if I could walk her back to the Holme. I proudly displayed her as we walked towards the exit. That feeling

of elation I will never forget, it replaced the previous hurt and it continued as we chatted earnestly on our way to the Inner Circle of the Park.

Jenna glanced up at the night sky. "Look what a beautiful night it is……...You can see the stars, aren't they pretty?"

"Like you," And then immediately regretted saying it. It sounded trite.

"Oh?" she said suspiciously. We were nearing the gate of the Holme.

"Can I take you out one night, there's a new film on at the Leicester Square cinema?"

"The Graduate? Yes that's great." We made the arrangements. Just before turning to go I leaned over to attempt a kiss. She responded. All around the dim white light from the old-fashioned streetlamp played patterns through the branches of the trees. It was a brief but happy moment. She turned to run the final few yards along the path to the doorway and then she was gone.

All the way home I was smiling. I smiled at the ticket inspector at the tube station. I smiled at the passengers sitting opposite on the train. I even smiled at Aaron in the morning at breakfast. There was no feeling of contempt at this breakfast time.

It would be a few days before I would see her again. We met in the college coffee lounge and chatted cosily, like we had known each other for years. Things seemed to be developing. At the cinema we stood close together as we waited in the queue to get in. The buskers readily entertained, parading to and fro along the pavement. It all seemed very comfortable and easy. We had a similar sense of values and could speak easily about seemingly all manner of topics, although I didn't attempt any conversation about science. Experience was telling me that science and romance did not mix. Another film, Midnight Cowboy, was showing soon which provided the perfect excuse to ask her out again. It was after seeing this film that she invited me to come around to the Holme for coffee the next day.

Promptly, the following evening, I arrived at the large black doors of this imposing residence. Situated within the center of the park it stood as a monument to the period of opulence that once was Great Britain. It was a large white house, best compared to a traditional manor house, built in the style of the architect Nash. The house was now converted to hold a limited number of female students and provided space for the Italian and English Departments. It had its own private grounds and was situated adjacent to both the college and the large lake within the park. I pushed the small doorbell. It seemed so small and insignificant against the tall Romanesque pillars and palisade adorning the whole front of this grandiose building. As I waited, I could hear the occasional shout of a girl's voice. "I'll get it!" said one. "Is there someone at the door?" said another. Finally, the door opened. It wasn't Jenna. It was a tall thin girl whom I didn't recognise. "Yes?" she asked.

"I've come to see Jenna Sanderson."

"It's for Jenna," she shouted, and then upstairs another voice carried on the message. Again, finally, Jenna appeared, the sound of her footsteps echoing on the wooden surface of the landing. She stood at the top of the stairs.

"Come on up." She beckoned with a confidence that

suggested she could have lived there for years. I began my assent, every board creaking underfoot as I went. After the splendid open staircase, we entered a corridor area. A small annex, to the left, housed a solitary girl ironing. Another annex, to the right, had been temporarily employed as the coffee area.

"Ah, coffee," I noted as we passed.

"Yes, I'll be back to get you one," she said firmly. We then came to a small landing hallway with five doorways. "This is my room here." She opened one of the doors and showed me in. "Have a seat, make yourself comfortable." It was a small narrow room with a bed, a sink, a tiny dressing table and a chair. I sat down on the bed and watched her moving around me as she searched for a coffee cup. I was enchanted by her presence. Just to have her so near was an amazing pleasure. "I promised you a coffee….so I'd better get on with it and make you one." Again, with a smile. "Shall I put on a record?"

"Yes, of course, anything."

"You're easy to please."

"Back in a mo'." Jenna disappeared outside to the coffee room. I sat and stared at the room and its contents. I missed her already. A small window indicated we were somewhere at the roof or attic level. Outside, only the tops of the trees were visible. I decided to see what was happening in the coffee area. Jenna was chatting to the girl who was ironing. To my surprise I recognized her. It was Lauren, Miss Prim. In an assured voice she introduced me and then carried on chatting until the coffee was ready. The two cups were placed with a clatter on a tray and carried back to her room.

"Is it ok for you to have someone in your room like this?" beginning to feel a little conspicuous.

"Yes, I think so," she answered thoughtfully.

"How many are you here?"

"About eight, including Margret Bridgstone. She has a room across the hall."

My pulse quickened a little as I realised my supervisor sat so near. We both sat on the bed together sipping our coffee and listening to the music. She sat close to me. I ventured to place my hand on hers and then we held each other in a brief hug. There was a genuine warmth between us. Further developments were distinctly hampered by the absence of a convenient backrest. Sitting upright at the edge of the bed seemed distinctly awkward and the progression towards a more horizontal position seemed a giant step at this stage.

"Did you enjoy the music in the films the other night?" I ventured, whilst I could think of what to do next.

"You mean Simon and Garfunkel?"

"And Midnight cowboy," I added. "I thought they were special."

"Yes, they were both good," she confirmed.

"Can you sing?"

"I don't think so, not very well at least,"
"Is there any chance you might sing for me?" I asked hesitantly, "That is, if I bribe you."

"What here, now?" she said with a worried tone.

"No, no," I assured her, "I have a twin track tape recorder, a tune, but no singer."

"You play an instrument then?" she asked cautiously.

"I try, but I hope it won't come between us," I followed. "Next week or so, maybe we can have a go…I'd like to hear you."

"What's the bribe? You didn't say." I leaned over and tried to grab hold of her. We both fell back as she pretended to escape and lay at an angle across the bed. We lay there for some moments in silence just holding each other. I felt the soft texture of her dress and the warmth of her body beneath. The talking had stopped as she allowed me to explore the source of this excitement that was building within me. It all seemed so natural and beautiful. Gone were all the fears I had before. All that existed now was a sense of urgency and a hope that Jenna felt the same way.

"Don't you think you ought to take off my tights first," came a quiet plea for practicalities. Despite my blunders Jenna remained very affectionate as we held each other close.

***

The next day we had an informal arrangement to meet in College. By lunchtime, however, there were no signs of Jenna. I decided to go to the Holme to see if she was there. It was only a short walk away and within minutes I was at the main door. It was open and inside I could see the entrance hall was quite busy with students on their way to lectures. I made my way up the stairs to find the corridor and the poorly lit hallway. It seemed very quiet, save for the creaking floorboards, no one to ask or speak to. I suddenly felt like an intruder and wondered whether I should turn back. But I was anxious to see Jenna so, whether invited or not, I found the door and knocked.

"Come in." Her voice sounded unusually weak.

"It's me, I hope you don't……..." I stopped because there was Jenna sat in crouched position on the bed looking distinctly out of sorts.

"What's wrong?"

"It's him!"

"Who?" I asked in astonishment.

"A boy I was going out with at home. He's written me a letter," she said with an irritated voice.

"Oh," trying to take things in.

"We finished before I came down here to College. Now he's being nasty to me," she said, now almost crying. The letter was held crumpled in her hand.

"Shall I stay?" I enquired gently, feeling a little in the way. A feeling of insecurity crept into my mind as I heard more about this situation. I sat down close to her and our shoulders touched.

"I looked for you in college today."

"Oh, I'm sorry…I was on my way" she said insistently. "Are you going to see him again?"

"No,…..I don't think so." It was not convincing. "He's

being so nasty." I put my arm around her waist and she leaned her head on my shoulder.

"And I thought you were upset because you hadn't seen me this morning," I said jokingly, hoping she would smile.

"I do want to see you, you know," raising the pitch of her voice.

"Have you had your lunch yet?"

"No," she replied with a whimper.

"Then it's time to eat,"

"You're being nice to me."

"I told you at the dance I would be kind," I reminded her.

"And I didn't believe you, did I," she said plaintively.

"Why should you."

As we left the silence in the hallway was disturbed by a series of laughs and giggles coming from the room opposite. "No, now it's not like that," said a male voice at one stage, followed by another burst of laughing and audible chatter.

"Whose room is that?" I asked curiously.

"Lauren Wilson….I think she has Will with her."

"Ah Miss Prim," I thought to myself, "Then again maybe not so prim. I knew Will from our Geology group. As we walked away the door opened and Lauren appeared. She saw me and quickly dismissed my presence with a curt hello.

"Jenna," she continued, "Paul was looking for you earlier….He didn't leave a message." Lauren appeared to enjoy the moment.

"Thank you," said Jenna. I didn't ask but could only wonder who Paul was. Lauren disappeared back into her room. We made our way out of her digs and had lunch at a café on the campus grounds.

"How are you feeling now?"

"I'm fine," she said cheerfully.

"I know you are," I said.

She looked up at me and said politely, "You don't have to say these things to me."

Before I could reply a passing car splashed dirty water in our direction forcing us to move quickly out of the way. Jenna glared sternly at the driver.

Lunch over we walked together across the grounds outside the college. Being November, it was quite chilly and so we decided to return back inside the college. We entered via Tuke Hall and the hall was empty.

"You never did say if you would have a go at singing,"

"Ok if you want me to," said with a definite tone in her voice, "What did you have in mind?"

"Come with me now." I took her hand and guided her into the hall and towards the stage.

Jenna looked at the piano. "Play me something then, if you can."

"I'll try." I sat down at the large black, baby grand piano. Jenna moved towards the front of the stage and stared out at all the empty seats. I began with an old Beatles song and sang the words directly to her. "If I fell in love with you would you promise to be true…………………

As I finished, she looked at me with her big brown eyes and smiled.

"Who's Paul?" I asked. She looked surprised.

"He's from the Geography Department," she said tentatively. "A year ahead of me."

I took a deep breath. "Are you going out with him?" In asking the question I thought it, highly unlikely, since we had been together for so much of the time.

"No, but he wants me to," I was beginning to feel distinctly outnumbered. Here she was, debating over what now amounted to three or four different fellas in her life. How did she find the time? I played a chord on the piano and felt depressed, if not outrightly jealous at this sort of attention. The notes on the piano began to flow and a tune was starting to develop.

"There's nobody chasing after me," I thought to myself. An F to E minor sequence really began to feel quite interesting, "Just one more change in this part….and there's a basis for a tune," I was thinking.

"Do you have to play now?" interrupted Jenna with a slight irritation. I stopped immediately and then chastised myself for being so obedient.

"You know your trouble….you're spoilt for choice."

"What do you mean?" I suddenly thought the remark too forward and backed off. The pause, however, just gave it emphasis.

"I think I know what you mean and I'm not." Her voice wavered a little. There was another pause. Then she said, "Will you come round to the Holme with me this evening?" She spoke as if she really cared and I felt better.

"With pleasure," I said cheerfully, "but before any of that, will you at least sing me a few notes…..Are you ready?" She was and she was great.

After the song I went to find a telephone. They were kept near the entrance to the college and were often occupied. I needed to ring Brian Reid to ask about the tapes of my songs. Fortunately, one of the phones was free and he answered straight away.

"Hi, Brian. I'm ringing about the tapes."

"Ah, good. It's fortunate you called, I have an appointment for you with the Moody Blues." My heart started pounding. "When would be a good time for you?"

"Any time," I replied immediately, "tomorrow?" I said quickly, why wait, I thought.

"Ok, ring me back in an hour to confirm." He put the phone down. An hour later he confirmed it was ok and to meet at his office at 5.00pm. In the excitement of the moment I put the phone down without asking what it was about. Of course, I spent the remainder of the day wondering.

"Maybe they are interested in recording the songs?" I said to myself. "Perhaps they want me in the band?"

The rest of the day went very slowly and it was difficult to concentrate on the lectures, especially since it was mineralogy. This was a subject I needed to pay more attention to. But I didn't. All I did was check my watch until finally it was 4.00pm and the lecture finished. Immediately I made my way to the tube station and then on to Brian's office. Suddenly I felt panicked. I had not brought my guitar. Sheepishly I entered the office. Brian was talking earnestly to a tall, well dressed, man in a suit with longish dark black hair. Brian eventually turned to me.

"Are you ready," he said abruptly.

"Yes," I was waiting for a comment about the lack of a guitar. None came.

"Okay Tony, lead the way," said Brian.

I followed, without a clue as to where I was going, or who this tall guy was. Was this something to do with the Moody Blues? It was dark and we got into a large BMW. I sat at the back afraid to interrupt their conversation. In fact, I couldn't really hear what they were talking about. We drove for about an hour through the city and out into the countryside. Not knowing the outer reaches of London, I hadn't a clue where I was when we stopped at a large country house. When we left the car, it was very dark as we made our way into the house. Inside, a grand hall had been converted into a studio. Several of the band members were there. They said "hi" and began setting up to play. I felt so intimidated by the cool atmosphere. Nobody was really making any conversation. I interpreted this as the "cool" way to behave in a famous band. Or maybe they had just had a big argument. Either way, after all this time in the car, I found it difficult to ask at this late moment why am I here. Especially, since I had no idea of their names. How stupid would I sound if I said, "Who are you?" Then suddenly I recognized a face. It was Justin Hayward, the only name I knew in the Moody Blues, who then immediately left.

Finally, one of the band handed me a guitar and said politely.

"What do you want to do?"

I so wanted to do the right thing. But what did they expect?

"How about you make up a song for us?"

This was risky, very risky but I so wanted to please. It was an acoustic guitar but there was an upright piano there as well. I suggested I play the piano.

"Sorry, that's not possible," he said with a smile on his face. The tall guy Tony, who I now assumed must be the manager, came over and opened up the piano lid.

"It looks like a normal piano, doesn't it," he began, and then took away the front panel, which revealed a row of tapes that you would use on a standard tape recorder. He then played the note C on the piano which made the sound of a violin. "All the tapes play the notes you would expect a normal piano to play but instead you hear the sound of a violin. When you play all the appropriate notes you can make it sound like an orchestra. We call it a Melotron."

He seemed really pleased with it.

"I didn't realise there was such an instrument," trying to look impressed. Inwardly, at this particular moment, I would have preferred a normal piano.

"It was our own idea," he said with pride. "We can use it on your song".

"No pressure then."

He smiled.

I played a possible introduction on the guitar and suddenly a melody emerged. Even the lyrics seemed to flow naturally out of the tune.

"Long time ago, we had a love,
As fresh as the breeze, bright as the sun,
But now that you're gone, look at the pouring rain."

I don't know where it came from but at least I had something to show. Sure enough, they used the Melotron for the backing track. The meeting was now brought quickly to close and I was sent home in a taxi. I still didn't know any more about why I was there and to this day I never found out. All I know is that there was no follow up with the Moody Blues. Nevertheless, not all was lost.

A week later I visited John at his office again purely to have a chat. No sooner had the conversation started when it was interrupted by a phone call. He answered, and after short discussion he looked over at me.

"Yes, he is here." said John, and then beckoned me to go to the piano. I shrugged my shoulders and went to stand by the piano. John put his hand over the mouth piece of the phone.

"I have the Tyne Tees TV on the line here and they need a theme tune for their new children's program called Zig Zag. It's due to air on Saturday and they have forgotten to arrange a Theme Tune for the program. Can you compose a tune now so we can play it over the phone?"

A little bemused but excited I sat down to play. Not knowing what would appear I began by striking the piano quite hard with the chord of C minor. My thumb was free to straddle the base note of F sharp and A major. As I rocked them backwards and forwards in a crisp 2/4 time the main rhythm and tune was born. A more complex and subtle middle eight break gave the tune depth and quality. The theme was done! It took just minutes. John was still on the phone and readily placed the receiver nearer the piano.

"How about this!" he said enthusiastically. Still on the phone he looked over at me. I dutifully played the melody again.

"How are you fixed for a trip up to Newcastle? They want to record the tune." I eagerly nodded yes.

"When?" I asked.

"How about now?"

The next day we were in the Tyne Tees studio. John introduced me to a band called The Foggy Tyners. They were famous for their hit song "Fog on the Tyne". They were going to provide the backing. I stood staring at a rather tired looking piano. I sat down on a small wooden stool and tried a few notes. Disappointingly, the keys were loose which took away the possibility to put in the attack required for the melody to sparkle. I looked up at John. He could tell there was something missing. Fortunately, as I played, the band filled in and with a sense of relief John seemed satisfied. But I was not. Nevertheless this was the recording that went out on TV the next day and so Zig Zag was born.

***

It was December 10th, nearing the Christmas vacation, and time to plan our return home. I never suffered pangs of homesickness, although when I did go home it was good. Jenna and I spent much of our time together and were becoming more and more inseparable. I thought less about the music and even less about my previously favorite scientific topic concerning DNA. Jenna was certainly not interested in this topic at all and could become quite agitated when the subject was raised. "Why are we here?", "Where are we going to?", "What is the purpose of life?" These were all questions being asked by everybody. Yet, curiously, if one ventured to explain some of these questions, and the way we behave, with respect to our DNA the response could be almost hostile and at best indifferent. It seemed everyone preferred their own explanation, often without reference to credible scientific thinking, more often veering towards religious fervor. Most looked towards external forces controlling everything. A God or benevolent omnipotent being which could look over us and protect us; that our destiny was somehow predetermined or that it could be altered or perhaps controlled. In fact, it was a dangerous area to raise during conversation. Without any effort I could find myself stood before a person I previously thought rational who was now in a full emotional discharge of anger. To interrupt such speeches with alternatives, was distinctly hazardous. In fact this actually happened on a field trip to the Isle of Arran.

Whilst we were there and after a dinner a group of us had

gathered into a small bar. Our discussions eventually entered into philosophical thoughts about life and its meaning. Our renowned Professor Reeves was there listening in. When I brought up the possibility of DNA control, the Professor became agitated and angry, announcing I needed to grow up and proceeded to wax lyrical about the importance of self-sacrifice. Such instances made me more cautious. I still wanted to develop the threads of ideas I had been puzzling in my head, but in these circumstances the whole subject was becoming an internal affair; something I kept to myself. Nevertheless, I still believed that the DNA possessed something very special and that at some stage I would pursue it further.

Jenna opened the door of the Holme and let me in. She was wearing my favourite maroon dress and as she climbed the stairs I stared admiringly at her shapely legs. She turned around.

"I hope you're not looking up my skirt, Nicholas Townsend," she said in a stern but joking manner.

"Of course I am!"

"I've told you about that…I don't like you doing that," she said with a note of insistence.

"Spoilsport!" As I caught up, I held her waist and she kissed me. We continued down the, now familiar, corridor. "What are your parents like?"

"Why?"

"Well it's nearly time to go home for Christmas," I paused as we entered her room "Or won't you be introducing me to your parents?" I asked in a way that said, "How important am I to you?" Once we were in the room Jenna responded.

"My father has his own small business making hair shampoo. He supplies many of the local shops," she began, "his passion, however, is Egyptology. He even gives lectures," she said proudly. This surprised me. He sounded interesting. "My mother just dotes on him. She is a very hard worker and looks after us all very well…..I also have an older brother. He's the black sheep of the family. That's because he wouldn't join in with dad's business. His wife is not really on speaking terms with the family." There was a pause. "Would you like to come and meet my parents?"

"Do you think it's wise?" It was partly a joke and partly not. "They are bound not to like me."
"You will come though, won't you?" she asked earnestly.

"How do you wish to travel *up north*?" I asked, "I usually thumb a lift…. You know at the start of the M1 at Hendon corner……Do you fancy that? It will save money." Saving money was important.

"Ok, I'll give it a go," she replied.

"And obviously you will come to meet my parents," I said almost threateningly.

"Now I don't think that would be wise at all." Spoken with a smile.

She picked up the ubiquitous coffee mugs and disappeared to the coffee area. I sat on the edge of the bed looking around the room. Sewing materials were in evidence everywhere together with a partly finished dress, draped over the top of the chair. Jenna came back in the room with the two coffees and placed them purposefully down on the table. Everything was done with purpose and clarity. I am always amazed by people who can do this. Their every action is direct and deliberate and without hesitation. It contrasted so much with myself who could lose contact with reality during the simple process of standing up. In my mind I was always somewhere else; never thinking about what was in front of me. Jenna sat down next to me and almost by reflex we gently put our arms around each other.

"Are you going to stay the night as we discussed?" she asked soulfully. Almost embarrassed, I nodded.

"I told Gary….so everything is ok back at the digs." I added. The time grew closer to 11.00pm and outside the sound of movements and distant voices grew less frequent. Finally, we heard Will leave with the usual accompaniment of chuckles and chatter.

"Goodnight Lauren," he said with a distinct northern accent, "..and don't throw that at me….and don't throw me down the stairs….I'm only human you know," Their voices grew fainter. After waiting a few more minutes we began to prepare ourselves in silence. I got into bed and watched her arrange her clothes on the chair. She knew I was watching her and pointed an angry finger at me as she turned to switch off the light. The bed was very small, so we held each other close and there we lay, arms around each other until the morning.

It was a Saturday morning and I would have to remain in the room until it could be assumed, I might have arrived under more normal circumstances. I could hear Grace Bridgstone speak in the distance. We had to remain silent the whole time. Finally, a suitable moment arrived. We furtively left the room accompanied by a chorus of creaking floorboards. Fortunately, our embarrassment was spared as we met no one in the corridor. No Will or Lauren either. I arrived at the front door with a great sense of relief. I took a deep breath of the fresh air and blinked, still a little startled by the bright morning light outside.

"See you Monday morning!" I said, "With your suitcase." I went directly back to the digs to pack.

When Monday arrived both Jenna and I made our way to Hendon Corner and took our place along a line of tramps and students. Almost immediately a car pulled up directly in front of us, carefully avoiding the others ahead in the queue and gestured insistently that we, and no one else, should get in. We were glad to do so. Hurriedly he sped off leaving behind the black looks and glares of those still waiting. Fortunately, he was on his way to Newcastle and took us all the way to Chesterfield. We said our farewells and arranged to get in touch again as soon as were home. I made the rest of my way back to Rotherham by bus. I became suddenly aware that this was the first time we had been apart since we had met. It was a curiously uncomfortable feeling.

With my suitcase in one hand and my guitar in the other I stepped off the bus. Rotherham now looked slightly unfamiliar to me. I stood momentarily and stared at the new Bus Station that had been completed since I'd been away. It was concrete as far as the eye could see. I didn't approve. I turned and walked awkwardly away towards my parent's house. It was only a short way, situated in a quiet cul-de-sac not far from the edge of the town. The street was lined on one side with small Victorian houses all showing the signs of neglect. On the other side was a large brick edifice referred to as the Tenement Hall but had long since fallen into disuse and was used primarily as a training center for the Sea Cadets. In my younger days I remember joining briefly, mainly because it was there, and other boys had done so. I had not the faintest idea what it was about, particularly since Rotherham was so far from the sea, and that everybody was so in earnest about a boat that was simply not there. I must have been very young. The building looked run down and in disrepair. Windows were broken and I remembered that at night it was a rather eerie place to walk around. In the adjacent narrow passageways and entrances rats were regularly sighted.

Next to it was yet another hall which had been converted into a garment factory. Along a short outside wall, the machinists, all ladies, sat and drank tea, smoked their cigarettes and noisily gossiped. It was always a gauntlet I had to negotiate whenever you entered or left the street. They were not adverse to shouting out embarrassing remarks as you walked by. Today they were not there, and I was able to pass by without event. A little further stood a long high and crumbling brick wall which extended down the rest of the street to our house. The house stood alone and detached. However, there was a garage area to one side which my father used for his car repair business. There he could be found almost any time of the day or week, working. He worked almost continuously and alone. As I made my way past the open doorway, I could catch a glimpse of my father's silver hair glinting in the murky light of the garage as he crouched down by a car, hammering hard.

"Hello Dad!" I shouted.

"Ah hello," he said in surprise. "Everything alright?"

"Yes!" I shouted enthusiastically.

"Your mother's in the kitchen."

"OK," I said, and that was the end of our reunion.

My father hardly ever indulged in small talk. He was a conscientious, proud man, a little serious and occasionally severe, as all good fathers should be of course. His lack of conversation however, would be unnerving, always leaving you feeling unsure and uncertain. You had to get to know his silences. Silences he had turned into an art form. He got his way most times without uttering a word. Why spoil things by talking. So, not wishing to change the pattern of a lifetime I paused only briefly, politely acknowledging how busy he was and then moved on towards the house. I opened the gate to a small front garden. The black and white paintwork of the gate was flaking off rapidly and the exposed wood beginning to rot. The little garden was full of weeds. I walked up a narrow passageway between the garage and the house. At the end I was met by a tall wood and iron gate. It made a familiar squeak and groan as it opened and closed; a sound I had heard a thousand times before and it made me feel at home. The gate had been made by my father as had many items about the house. He had made furniture, cupboards, the television set, the television aerial, the wireless set; even the concrete path I stood on had been laid by him. His technical abilities were endless. I turned towards the back door of the house glancing briefly at the patchy lawn. It was mainly tufts of rough grass with only a few weeds for flowers. Two tall plain trees provided a welcome touch of real nature as they rustled majestically at the bottom of the garden. I turned again towards the house. My mother stood smiling at the kitchen window, her spectacles glinting as they caught the last of the late afternoon light. She was beginning to look old. She wore her usual slightly worried expression that suggested the world might end tomorrow. This was my mother's weapon which she could use to get her own way. Consequently, family life could often be father sitting in his chair staring at the fire in stony silence whilst mother looked on anxiously. I put down my suitcase and guitar in a small porchway by the door and entered the house.

"You've come home then," said with a little sarcasm.

"Until January," I replied. Making it sound like an eternity. I brought in the suitcase.

"No doubt that's full of dirty washing," she said with a sigh. It wasn't, but I wouldn't explain that yet. The kitchen table had a neat pile of freshly ironed clothes and several more hung from a rack near the ceiling.
"Have you said hello to your father?"

"Yes, we have met before," I said sarcastically.

"He doesn't like it when you walk past without saying hello."

"He still doesn't say very much."

"I know, but he likes you to make an effort," she said in his defence. "What do you want for your tea?" The telephone rang.

"I'll get it," I said, and then shouted "Poached egg on toast would be nice". I moved to the hall and answered the phone. It was Jenna.

"Are you OK?" she said spritely.

"Yes fine,…..Are you…..What are we going to do …… Can't wait to see you again…..How about meeting up somewhere?" I asked.

"Well there's a party tomorrow night you could come to. My old boyfriend asked me to go to his party. He's having lots of old school friends and said to bring you along. too".

There was a pause. I didn't like the sound of this. The old boyfriend was still in control. My eyes became fixed on the wall in front of me as her words rattled brusingly around inside. I felt hurt and was trying desperately not to admit it.

"Why is she doing this to me?" I thought, feeling sorry for myself. "After only a few hours away and already I'm feeling like excess baggage…..I should leave her to go without me." But somehow, I knew that I would have to go if I really wanted to keep her.
"Are you still there?" she asked waiting for a reply.

"Where do I meet you?" I said without feeling.

Jenna continued enthusiastically, seemingly unaware of the significance of my indifferent reply.

"Come to the house first, you've got my address………… Will you get the car?"

"I don't know…..I would think so," I said, recovering a little. We continued talking. My mother walked down the hall looking enquiringly as she passed. I put down the phone.

"Was that one of the Brians'? she asked. There were two former school friends called Brian. Sometimes it seemed everyone in my life was called Brian.

"No. It was Jenna, a girl I met at college. She lives in Chesterfield. We came back up together. Do you think dad will let me borrow the car tomorrow?"

"I don't know, you'd better ask him yourself,"

I went into the dining room, switched on the television

and sat down. I rarely watched television in term time, so this would be a novelty. My mother entered the room.

"Where is all your dirty washing?"

"In my suitcase,"

"I've just looked in there. There's not very much. Don't tell me you've started looking after yourself." she said disbelievingly.

"No not really."

"I don't think so either," she emphasised. "Has that girl been washing your things?" she asked curiously.

"Some of them," trying to play the importance down. Nothing further was said as she returned into the kitchen. My thoughts were returning to Jenna again. Confused and irritated, I sat quietly trying not to fidget. I would have to wait until tomorrow evening.

My mother brought in the poached egg, so I sat down to eat. It wasn't long before my father came in from the garage dressed in his paint stained overalls. He began to consume his cheese on toast in a noisy manner. I hurried to finish and escape.

"How is Rotherham United at the moment?" I asked to open the conversation.

"Hmph," he replied with a sort of grunt.

"Have you been down to watch?" We lived close to the football ground.

"It's not worth it these days," he replied, as though they

personally owed him a trophy or two.

"Do you remember when our dog joined in the game against Cardiff City,"

"Hmph," he replied.

"I can still see him being chased by the players. I shouted look dad it's… and you put your hand over my mouth".

"Your mother says you've got a girlfriend?" He never referred to my mother by name,

"Yes, I think so," I replied doubtfully.

"What's her name?"
"Jenna, she's local. I'm hoping to see her tomorrow night. Can I borrow the car?" I asked hopefully and without further presumption he agreed.

It seemed I would go to the ball after all. It was a familiar and local route.

The car came to a halt. It was dark and I hesitated before entering. I decided to continue and drove up a short, inclined driveway to park at the side of the house. It was a large white house with unusual shapes, arches and corners. The gardens at the front and back seemed large and formal, surrounded by high hedges of copper beech with speckled gold as they caught the car lights. The weather was distinctly inclement. I knocked on the door and wondered about her parents. No reply. This time I knocked a little louder and within seconds a light appeared in the adjacent window. The door opened.

"Yes?" said a man in a slightly affected voice.

"I've come to see Jenna," I said politely, "is she in?" He was not very tall, in his late fifties with dark receding hair. His eyes were small, a feature that seemed exaggerated by the old fashioned pair of spectacles he wore.

"Wait there a few moments would you please" he said very formerly, again in the same affected tone and almost with disdain. It felt like I'd come to the tradesmen's entrance and was being treated accordingly. He turned almost regally and disappeared. Meanwhile the rain began to fall, and I stepped closer to the open door for shelter as I waited. Jenna finally arrived.

"Hello, come in," she said with a welcoming voice. "I'm nearly ready. Come through." She took me through a large kitchen into a hall which had a large ornate grandfather clock standing at the foot of the stairway. She paused to look at me before we went into the living room.

"I'll introduce you."

The living room was large and divided in two parts by a central fireplace and open archway either side. It was tastefully decorated with small flower patterns and dark wooden furniture. We walked through to where her parents were watching television. Her mother sat knitting. She was slim but with a homely appearance.

"I'll be back in a moment." Jenna disappeared upstairs.

"Do sit down," said her mother with an amused smile.

I wondered what had amused her. Her father was sat opposite and didn't move or turn to look at me. They continued to watch the television. To my surprise it was football.

"Is it a good match?" I asked, trying to make conversation.

"Oh, I'm not watching it," said her mother. "I don't enjoy watching these things," she said with disdain. "Footballers are just morons really".

"Oh dear," I pondered. "I wonder what that makes me". There was a silence.

"And what do you do?" asked her father begrudgingly. "I'm studying Geology."

"Is that useful?" he asked patronisingly.

"It can be. The evolution of the earth has always interested me… hills, valleys. The formation of new mountains, new oceans…"

"New ones," he interrupted with surprise, "there won't be any new ones." he said correcting me. "These valleys and hills have always been here and always will".

"Of course they will," confirmed her mother. I was a little bemused.

"You won't be too late will you?" she continued, as Jenna returned.

Finally, Jenna was ready, and we left. My first meeting with her parents had been distinctly odd if not icy. In contrast Jenna looked warm and very attractive. It was so good to see her again and I wanted to tell her so, but other thoughts prevented me. Unfortunately, I was thinking of the impending party and the likely confrontation with her previous boyfriend.

"Are you looking forward to the party?" I asked.

"It will be nice. I'll see lots of old schoolfriends"

"What's he like your old boyfriend?"

"I shan't be bothered about talking to him at all," she said unconvincingly.

We arrived and I wondered why I was there. He met us at the door, showed us in, put his arm around her and then immediately began a private conversation. Jenna introduced me. He was everything I didn't want him to be, tall, well-built, good looking with relatively short fair hair. Worst of all he seemed assured and self-confident. Mind you, relative to me, even the hat stand next to me had more authority and confidence.
"Go through Nick," he instructed, "I've got something I'd like to show Jenna."

"Oh yes," I said unbelievingly. This whole situation was an idiotic mistake. I looked accusingly at Jenna and disappeared on my own into one of the rooms to get a drink, which I drank far too quickly and then I got another. Jenna returned within minutes. She looked slightly upset.

"What was that about?" I asked with an obvious tone.

"Nothing really. He was returning a present of mine. Look, he's not important anymore. He's got a new girlfriend."

Everything she said was obviously hurting her as much as me.

"Let me get you a drink," I said changing the subject.

"OK, and then I'll introduce you to Boris."

Boris had a bushy dark beard and was very friendly. What a relief. We chatted happily for a while until it was time for more drinks. I volunteered and went to the kitchen. In a more buoyant mood, I stood at the array of bottles in front of me. Two individuals leaning against the window stared at me a little more intently than required.

"What a lot a bottle," I said attempting to interrupt the silence, "Do I help myself?"

"If you're capable," said one of the pair icily. I began to pour some wine.

"You're Nick aren't you?" he started. "Jenna's new boyfriend?"
I became aware of the third person behind me.

"You're a bit of a berk aren't you Nicholas?" said the person behind me.

It was Jenna's old boyfriend. He came closer towards me in an intimidating manner. "She's a good screw you know."

I was angry now. Before I knew what I was doing, I turned away, lifted my arm and without hesitation rammed my elbow hard into his stomach. I felt it sink in and strike his ribs. He reeled backwards and fell awkwardly onto a chair and then the floor. My knees turned to jelly.

"Oh, dear I am sorry," I said, "I didn't see you there".

His two friends tried to reach me across the table but fortunately they were effectively blocked in. They looked angry. Before he recovered, I picked up two glasses of wine in my trembling hands and left quickly, and with my heart still racing, I returned.

"Boris would you mind getting the beers. I couldn't find them?" I was still feeling my hands tremble slightly.

Jenna didn't seem to notice, probably assuming it was my usual nervousness in company. Mark came into the room and glared at me, then disappeared upstairs. "Not the best host I've encountered." I mused. Boris returned without comment and handed over the beer. I stood there waiting for something to happen…..but it didn't and slowly I began to feel better. There were no repercussions and soon it was time to leave. As we approached the door a voice called to Jenna and I was left alone for a few minutes. Without warning I felt someone grab my arm and then the pain as it was worked behind my back. It was Mark.

"Don't ever try that again, do you hear."

"Maybe you should try being a better host," I replied.

Another couple came into the hall and he quickly let go and went back upstairs before he could do any real damage. Jenna returned and we left.

It was still raining and we had to dash over to where the car was parked. Once inside the windows seemed to steam up quickly.

"Home James," said Jenna. "Did you enjoy the party? I told you everything would be alright".

She didn't see my expression.

"I want you, not him." She sounded more certain.

I felt better.

"Do we have to go straight home?" I said, suggesting a small diversion, she took hold of my arm. This time I didn't mind my arm being held at all.

CHAPTER FOUR

Once again, I made the now familiar journey back to London. As per usual I was the first to arrive and it was late. In the absence of company, I went straight to bed.

In the morning I felt the cold damp air on my face as I awoke. I opened my eyes to stare at the unfamiliar bedroom, forgetting for a moment where I was. The damp chill in the air followed me as I made my way to the bathroom. I perused the new wash basin as I brushed my teeth. I made my way downstairs and was astonished to see Aaron was already sat at the breakfast table. He didn't look up or greet me.

"Hello," I said, far too generously.

"Hello," he said, without expression.

I waited for him to continue but nothing further was said. I ventured again.

"Did you have a good vacation?"

"Not particularly," he replied with precision. He lifted his head and without turning to face me, continued to look straight ahead. His eyes moved suddenly to the side to stare directly at me.

"Did you?" he asked coldly and lingered more than was necessary on each word. I sat there a little bemused by this display. Aaron was quite a character. What type of character, however, was debatable.

"Not bad," I answered, "I did have a party. There were quite a few from college came. It was good," I said trying to be nonchalant.

In fact, the party wasn't good, it was an unmitigated disaster, but I wasn't going to tell Aaron that. Gary came, and between us we tried to breathe some life into it but to no avail. It seemed outside of college none of these students wanted to talk to each other. I tried to put the whole thing out of my head only to be brought back to the attentions of Aaron.

"You came in late last night," he said accusingly. "Not exactly a good start is it?"

"Good enough." I said tersely. Then I suddenly realised that Aaron was in the house yesterday, keeping silent, holed up in his little room. That seemed typical.

Aaron's personality intrigued me. His cutting edge was poignant and effective as well as hurtful. It seemed controlled and executed with precision. But why so much of his everyday conversation was so venomous I could never understand. I imagined him having a cruel father and wicked stepmother. Perhaps he had been taunted by the ruthless antics of an elder brother. In reality, I doubted any of this was likely. He was just very adept at being nasty. He appeared to make few friends, if any. Or did he? His anemic gaunt appearance was made even more sour by his manner, not at all attractive. Everything seemed stacked against him and deliberately so. He clearly chose to act in this way. But what on earth was the gain in doing this." I took another look at him. He ate his breakfast maintaining the same gaunt profile, straight back and upright head, employing mechanical short sudden movements to raise the food to his mouth. I continued to ponder. Aaron glanced at my attentions suspiciously.

Perhaps he didn't make the sort of friendship I understood, but I had to concede what he did gain was a kind of respect. At this stage no one was rushing to befriend him but, then again, they didn't cross him either. I'd also noticed another thing. Whenever we all sat around the table for breakfast or lunch and Aaron decided to go into action (in the oratory sense) for these moments Andy and Brian would figuratively stand behind him."

With this in mind, I suddenly stared directly at Aaron in astonishment. He must have noticed the strange look that had appeared in my eyes and immediately leered back at me. Nothing was said.

Until this moment I had dismissed Aaron's behavior as just generally unpleasant. Now I suddenly saw it as a shrewd and clever strategy. I chastised myself for ever entertaining a complimentary thought about him. Nevertheless, I was quite envious and even a little jealous. As each thought occurred I was drawn to look at him but tried desperately to resist. Ironically it was Aaron now that was beginning to look uncomfortable. He seemed to hurry the last few morsels on his plate and left the table very quickly. An irritate Mrs. Carter stood before me. I hadn't noticed her enter the room.

"What did you say?" she said in astonishment.

"Admiration!" I said firmly staring straight at her.
"Hmph, shouldn't you be at college," she said, looking slightly flustered.

I'd given Aaron far too much of my thinking time this morning, so I quickly went upstairs for my coat and bag. I journeyed alone to college. The main hallway was a hive of activity. There was no sign of Aaron, thank goodness. A familiar voice interrupted.

"Which sexy blonde have you got your eye on?" It was Gary.

"Hey!" I exclaimed, glad to see him, "I've got my eyes on all of them, of course."

"You'll go blind….You should wear sunglasses." followed Gary.

"Fancy a cup of coffee?"

We moved off towards the lounge area.

"Just arrived?" he asked.

"Yes, another term begins," I said, registering the moment. "I've just put my case in the lobby……And you?"

"Arrived yesterday…….Aaron is already here,"

"Oh great," he said sarcastically, "thanks for the reminder….I just saw Andy in the corridor."

"No signs of Brian then?" I said, accounting for everybody. Gary stared straight at me. His expression had changed.

"He's dead, Nick……Didn't you know?" I looked at him in stunned silence. "Towards the end of the vacation he was taken into hospital complaining of headaches and nausea. Within a few days he was dead."

"You're joking?"

"They operated…..they believed it was a brain tumor," he said somberly.

"But he was fine….there was nothing wrong with him!" My eyes were beginning to water.

"But there was nothing wrong with him," I repeated in a form of protest.

Gary continued to explain.

"I found out from Monica because she was a friend of his girlfriend."

"Girlfriend? I didn't know he had a girlfriend," I said looking up in surprise. It just showed how little I really knew him. Nevertheless, I was shocked. The morning coffee passed rather quietly. I made my way towards the first lecture still with the shock of Brian ringing in my head. Looking up I saw Toby, an amiable but important character of the geology group.

"You look as though you need vacation" he said observantly. "The thought of work has the same effect on me," he said jokingly and walked on. He wasn't interested in a reply.

Actually, his comment was correct in a way. It was a Biology practical I was heading for, and the sight and smell of a dissection, I could do without at this moment. I was, in fact, looking forward to meeting Jenna afterwards. We had arranged to meet for lunch. The practical lasted forever. Afterwards in my rush to get to the refectory I bumped into Gary again.

"Are you over the shock of Brian yet?"

I nodded. We decided to get some food and keep a look out for Jenna. Trying to find a place to sit I saw James, Toby and Steve Langley and suggested we join them. As I sat, I felt tired, unusually tired. I could still smell the formalin from the dissection. It was a sickly penetrating odour which always lingers for hours afterwards. Gary sat opposite. He studied physics so he didn't really know any of the Geology crowd. I tried re-introducing him.

"You remember Gary." I said in an almost embarrassed tone. I was never very good at doing introductions. There was a pause.

"We're thinking of renting a flat," said Toby finally breaking the silence, "do you fancy joining us?"

I was flattered they had asked. "Sounds like a good idea." I replied. I thought about Gary and looked over towards him, but these were not really his friends. I left it at that. Peter appeared and sat himself down next to me.

"Hey!" I squeaked, "I was saving that seat for Jenna."

"Have you asked Nick about the Folk Club?" said Peter remaining seated.

"Nope," said Toby, "We've asked him about the flat but not about the Folk Club."

"What's all this about, then?" I asked suspiciously.

"Don't look so worried Nick. We know you would love to do it," said James tauntingly.

"Do what?" I asked exasperatedly.

"Start a Folk club of course......We sort of volunteered you for the job" said Peter with a mock expression of concern. Jenna entered the refectory and quickly walked up to us.

"What do you think, Jenna?" I asked with a smile.

"Not very much." she replied irritably, "where am I supposed to sit?"

I leaned forward to get up but to my surprise fell back feeling faint. My legs seemed so weak.

"Are you going to get up for me or not?" Her tone was demanding. She was obviously put out by the fact I was supposed to meet her and I appeared otherwise occupied. I managed to stand up on the second attempt but felt a pain in my legs. Jenna sat down and I sat on the corner of the table close to her. Suddenly she looked up at me and said very loudly, "You smell disgusting!!" A girl close by immediately turned and stared at me with a disapproving expression. Peter and Steve laughed.

"Thanks," I said sarcastically without explaining the formalin.

"They've asked Nick to start a Folk Club….What do you reckon Jenna?" said Gary trying to get the conversation back on course. Jenna didn't say anything. Despite my obvious interest in such a project, the thought of it worried me a little. Although I had an instinctive feel for all kinds of music, I had no special interest or experience with Folk music. I certainly had no experience at all in organising such things.

"He can do what he likes," said Jenna rather indignantly. It sounded abrupt and uncaring. Somehow nothing pleased her. To avoid a further escalation I opted for the meek way out.

"I'd need Jenna's organising skills," I said, "Without that support there's no way I'll manage it." It sounded insipid.

"Why did I do that," I thought tersely to myself.

"That's a great idea," said Steve. Jenna smiled at last and I was relieved.

"Looks like a 'Fait a compli', I said picking up my plate. I turned to Jenna "I think we had better go and get some fresh air." We left and walked towards the park.

"Have you got any more lectures this afternoon?" asked Jenna.

"No," I replied curiously.

"Shall we go back to the Holme?" she said looking directly at me.

"I thought I smelled?"

"I know, I want you to go and have a bath."

"Hmph," I grunted disappointedly. She stood back and then opened her arms.

"Kiss me." I walked towards her and grabbed her around the waist.

"Hold your nose!" I suggested.

* * *

It was now fast approaching Easter and having accepted the task of setting up and running the Folk Club, the Summer Ball was fast approaching. Unfortunately, so were the exams. I decided to think about this a little whilst playing the piano in the large Tuke Hall. As always, a new song was in the making and in fact took most of my attention. It wasn't long, however, before I heard the distinctive sound of Jenna's footsteps striding purposely across the stage.

"I thought I'd find you here," said Jenna complainingly. "Don't forget we have to decide on the Summer Ball soon."

"What do you think of the Spinners as a name to pull in the crowd?"

In reality, they were not at all my taste and I was reluctant even to suggest the idea. It appeared they were a band everyone loved to hate, yet they could still attract the audiences.

"With the money we make we could afford the Strawbs the following week," I said hoping the point was made. "The Spinners are appearing this week in London with Georgie Fame…Shall we go and see them?"

"We could invite them to the College Ball at the same time….Do you know exactly where they're appearing?" asked Jenna.

"No…shall I see what I can find out then?"

"Ok, but will you come and eat now. You know you look so thin. I think you should see a doctor. You are definitely losing weight and those fainting spells you're having…." she said with an organised tone in her voice.

"Yes okay, but first I want you to hear my new song." It was a lively melodic tune designed to make you feel lighthearted. So, I began. I think she liked it.

The Spinners were appearing at a College nearby. We

made arrangements to be there at 8 o'clock. It was a typical College set up, having to walk through a maze of corridors before finally locating the hall where it was to be held. It was dimly lit but we could still make out that it was reasonably full already. This was an encouraging sign. Jenna looked up at me to notice the perspiration pouring down my forehead.

"You must see a doctor," she said with concern.

"I will…I promise,"

"I do love you," she said.

"Do you?" I said in almost disbelief. This was the first time anyone had said this to me. I felt honored. But strangely I could not bring myself to reply. The word seemed too big for a quick and glib reply.

"Shall we sit here?" said Jenna breaking the silence. We sat down to watch the show. Eventually the Spinners appeared. They were professional and impressive. The hall was completely full.

"It's busy but have they really come to see Georgie Fame?" I said, not convinced.

"Difficult to judge," said Jenna, "I don't like the Spinners really."

"Neither do I, but we are supposed to present folk musicians."

At the finish of their spot they disappeared off stage, so we got up to follow them. By the time we had reached the corridor there were no obvious signs of them. A single person stood over by the lift so we ventured over. His back was towards me.

"Excuse me did you happen to see the Spinners pass this way?" I asked politely. He turned. It was Georgie Fame. The lift arrived.

"Follow me," he said curiously. We stepped inside the lift and for a moment we stood not knowing what to say.

"We run the Folk Club at our College," I began, "we're hoping the Spinners might appear there." The words came out in an embarrassed way.

"Yeah, why not." he said with mild surprise.

We stepped out of the lift and he directed us down a corridor and then another. It felt just like a hospital with shiny cream painted walls and endless doorways. It seemed strange to see such a famous popstar in such clinical surroundings.

"This way,"

He finally opened one of the doors to reveal a lecture room. He didn't follow. It had been temporarily converted into a dressing room. The Spinners seemed everywhere. Clothes draped over benches, over stools; guitars propped up against any available wall or table. The Spinners themselves were still in their now traditional polo neck sweaters. Somehow, being this close, they appeared even more impressive. There were so many of them. Cliff Hall seemed the most approachable, so I ventured a few words and asked him if they might be interested in playing at our College. I didn't really know what to expect as a response. I suddenly thought we might be going about this bottom side up.

"Don't talk to me about such technical matters," he said with brevity, "you need to talk to our director." With a smile he pointed over towards the tallest of the group. On the stage he was the most outspoken. He was already staring down intently at some paperwork.

"May I speak with you a moment?" I asked tentatively. He turned and stared purposefully straight at me.

"What can I do for you sonny?" he said sharply. I was taken back by his briskness. I took a breath and began.

"Would you be interested in appearing at our College Summer Ball, and if so, what would be your rates?"

He stopped what he was doing and then moved closer towards me and putting his arm around my shoulder he said,

"Look, if you invited us to your College you will do very well."

Out of the corner of my eye I could see Jenna cringing at what was happening. He continued. "We will tell you what to charge and then give you a proportion of the takings."

I couldn't bare his manner. He stood very close and his voice was so patronising. Stepping back out of his reach I thanked him for his offer and said we would think about it. I took a business card he offered and left immediately with Jenna. I looked at the business card. I had never really seen one before.

"What a cheek!" exclaimed Jenna as soon as we were safely away, "and so smarmy with it." We returned to watch Georgie Fame. He was great.

LOCKED TOGETHER

The business of running a Folk Club actually brought me in touch with many well-known artists, especially when I became acquainted with the studios of the BBC radio program "Country Meets Folk". It was situated at the Playhouse Theatre by Charing Cross Bridge. Here, I was a regular visitor watching the show from the studio control room. It was at this time I met Wally Whyton, a celebrity country singer famous for various songs such as Leave Them a Flower. I was also well acquainted with the technical producer and spent most of my time in the Control Room at the rear of the theatre. It was there that I ventured to ask if I could apply to be a Production Assistant at the BBC. It was arranged and I attended several interviews at the BBC Television Centre, London. Unfortunately, I failed at the very last interview. It was with a high brow character who immediately took a dislike to my broad Yorkshire accent, as I did to his posh verbosity.

The next day I awoke back at the digs. My illness was taking a firmer hold. The bedclothes were damp with sweat and as I tried to move, I felt weak and my body ached. Even the smallest movement seemed difficult. I pushed back the bedclothes. A conspicuous cloud of steam rose and condensed from my pajamas. They felt heavy with sweat. I glanced over to the other bed looking for Andy. He wasn't there. Slowly I got myself dressed and prepared for breakfast. At the foot of the stairs I stumbled. Unfortunately, Mrs. Carter the landlady appeared at that moment with my breakfast. She looked at me coldly with her steely blue eyes and then stomped loudly into the lounge slamming the plate down with a clatter. In an instant she stomped out yet again without a word. It was nine thirty. Everyone else had left for lectures. I sat alone at the table and stared at the leathery egg and the fatty bacon glistening on the plate. I had no appetite but knowing Mrs. Carter, this lot had to disappear somehow. I took my handkerchief and with the knife and fork transferred the contents of the plate on to it. I lifted the handkerchief carefully, reached the hallway and paused to check the way was clear. To my horror the egg slid out, hitting the carpet and breaking open the yolk. Holding the bacon in one hand I tried in vain to clean up the up the spreading yolk with the handkerchief. I heard the approaching sound of footsteps. Desperately I tried, in the fading seconds, to finish cleaning up but instead it only got worse. Mrs. Carter appeared and then stopped in front of me, stared a fearsome stare and then strode angrily back into her kitchen. She reappeared within seconds.

"Get out!" she screamed. She moved aggressively towards me. "Get out!" she shouted again.

I was hot, ached and couldn't have escaped even if I'd wanted to. Standing up slowly I dragged myself up the stairs. Mrs. Carter shouted up the stairs after me.

"You find yourself other digs...do you hear." I heard but didn't answer.

Somehow, I managed to get to College but could only slump into one of the lounge chairs. I sat there, motionless, for some time. Eventually Jenna came to look for me. She walked over towards me.

"You're perspiring badly," she said anxiously, "Come on, we're going to a doctor."

I do not remember how we got there, only that I found myself sitting in a doctor's waiting room. To my surprise the doctor thought there was nothing wrong which made Jenna angry.

"Nothing wrong!" Jenna exclaimed to the doctor, "He can

barely move. He's ill. You've got to help him." The doctor seemed unimpressed and I was dismissed. I lurched slowly out of his room and then sat heavily on one of the waiting room chairs to rest. The persons sitting either side of me moved away.

"I'll get you back to the digs," said Jenna trying to be helpful.

"No don't do that," I said weakly, "she doesn't want me back there anymore."

"You have to go back. You're so ill."

"I feel so tired…I'm burning up," I mumbled.

Jenna helped get a taxi and we made our way back to the digs. She practically carried me to the front door and using my key we entered. Aaron was in the hallway to greet us. Not wishing to let an opportunity pass him by immediately commented. "Drunk again Townsend…I don't know how you put up with him," he said to Jenna.

"Not now Aaron," I mumbled again.

"He's ill. Can't you see!" said Jenna valiantly, almost convinced nobody was going to recognise what was going on. Mrs. Carter came out of the kitchen

"He's not going up there." She spoke firmly. "Get him out of here." Aaron immediately grinned one of his famous grins, picked up his bag and left. Jenna however stood firm.

"I'm taking him upstairs and then getting him a doctor." Ignoring Mrs. Carter we struggled upstairs and I collapsed on the bed. The outside world was beginning to fade. I could hear words faintly in the distance, "……he's not staying……." My body was in such turmoil. The noises in the room turned into music. It was fairground music and I could now see a fairground. I was spinning as free as a big Ferris wheel. The wheel went round and round and the more it went round the more I became the wheel and my whole body was twisting, turning and twisting. After that moment I remember very little. It was three months before I recovered and was able to return back to college. In that time the examinations came and went and so did the Summer Ball and many other events. Jenna looked after me until I was able to be moved home. She wrote to me regularly. When I returned, it was to the new flat at Queens Park with Peter, Toby and Steve Langley. I had lost so much weight that I couldn't sit for more than a few minutes without the aid of a cushion.

It wasn't long, however, before I was back into some sort of reasonable shape. Fit enough even for a night out with the boys. "Leave Jenna behind just for one night," said Steve persuasively, "we're going into London to try out a few pubs. We've been here nearly three years and never spent any time in London. It's time we put that right." I agreed immediately. Jenna, however, was not pleased. As the evening progressed it became evident that it was Steve's intention that we should also experience at least one striptease club. We made our way towards Soho and to a pub immediately which had opposite, an establishment which had naked girls displayed liberally around its doorway. From the relative safety of the pub lounge we stared out through the window at the wonderland of female flesh being offered tantalisingly on the display boards on the other side of the road. After a few lukewarm "Shall we", "Shouldn't we", we were on our way across the road heading for the entrance.

The entrance was a single doorway leading downstairs into

a small, dark theatre. There were several rows of seats but each row had only five or six seats. It was very quiet with only about six or seven other people in there. The curtain to the miniature stage was closed. We sat down with difficulty trying hard to behave in a more soberly manner.

"Come and sit down," said Peter, "hands out of pockets."

"I'm sure this seat is wet!" I remarked.

"That was quick," said Steve.

"Shh! Be quiet. I want to concentrate," urged Peter.

We all quietened down and waited for the start. The few dim lights went out. A strange crackling sound suddenly filled the room followed by a poor quality recording of rhythmic music. The curtain opened. The light from the stage lit up our faces. We stared intently. A young girl appeared scantily dressed and began a slow dance. She proceeded to undress which did not take long since she was wearing so very little in the first place. After she had finished the striptease, she stopped her attempt at dancing and sat herself on a high stool where she remained motionless. We continued to stare scutinising every curve that had been suddenly made available. The room was heavy with silence. Somehow, unfortunately, the sight of this naked girl didn't seem so interesting without movement. This state of affairs continued for a few minutes, without change until at some appointed moment she stood up and left the stage. Almost immediately an older, but still shapely, woman appeared and repeated the same routine. As she sat there on the stool, she suddenly stared directly at me and shouted, "What are you doing here son?" I was totally embarrassed and wanted to disappear down a crack in the seat. Peter, however, wasn't bothered at all and immediately played on the word "son".

"We've come to see you mother," he shouted back. Steve continued with the same theme.

"Mummy, why do you make us come here and watch you do this?" He said mockingly, "we want our dinner."

There was a giggle from the audience. The woman was not impressed and left giving us a two fingered gesture.

"Isn't she a nice lady," said Peter loud enough for the audience to hear.

"Let's go….I think Peter`s mum is really on next," said Steve getting anxious that we were about to be thrown out. We left trying to remember the way back. Although I had only consumed one pint of beer, my system really wasn't ready for any quantity of beer and was beginning to feel the worse for it. By the time we made it to Leicester Square tube station I wasn't feeling too great at all. I delicately stepped on to the tube hoping for the best. The motion of the train rolled us back and forth. I hung on to the handrail with a quiet desperation clinging also to the rapidly fading belief I could make it home. It was not to be, and I was gloriously sick where I stood. Fortunately, the noise of the carriage rattling along drowned the unpleasant sounds accompanying this display. In addition, I was stood at the far end of the carriage which attracted less attention as I looked down at the awesome pool before me. Unfortunately, it wasn't long before the movement of the train began to shift the fluid content down the central walkway of the carriage. Those passengers with their backs to me were not really, aware of what had gone on until out of the corner of their eye they glimpsed its progress past them like a free-flowing glacier. Despite the fact we were only travelling to Queens Park, the journey seemed to take forever and there was simply no escape. Peter and Steve disowned me and had moved by now to the opposite end of the carriage where they stood laughing. But it wasn't very funny at all. At long last the train pulled to a halt. Steve continued to laugh.

"Did you see the expression on their faces as it trickled down the carriage?"

"That was good ale you wasted there, Nick," continued Peter.

We began walking towards the flat when Peter suddenly changed the subject completely, and bluntly asked "Are you going to marry Jenna?" Without hesitation I replied.

"Yes, if she'll have me."

"Why don't you get married now?"

"I don't really know," I pondered. This was a question of marriage; a big question and I tried to think of why I couldn't answer more positively. "Perhaps it's because we are still young and there is no real necessity."

"When will it be a necessity?" asked Peter.

"When do you think it's necessary?" I said returning the question.

"Don't you want to live together?"

"We virtually are living together, aren't we?"

"What happens if someone else takes her?" persisted Peter.

"Aren't there more fish in the sea?" I said, which I regretted. It sounded cold and did not intend to be so glib.

The thought was wounding enough without the reality. "Anyway what about your longstanding relationship with Susan. Isn't there a question of marriage there?"

"Susan isn't ready yet," said Peter sheepishly.

"Oh," I said, regretting I'd asked, "you once told me that you'd already been in close relationships with others. Perhaps that's why you feel more certain…that you've got somebody special," I suggested weakly. "With Jenna I know it's good but how do I know it's special?"

"Is anything that special?" said Steve, who had been listening. "Take a beautiful building. In the beginning you recognise it to be an attractive house. Only later does it become a home….a special place. Something that special can only come with time."

"You'll be sixty before you're that certain," said Peter.

"There are some who believe you know straight away," I said with interest, "One look and you know."

"That's weird." remarked Steve, "How can anything so far reaching in your life be decided in an instant."

"Love at first sight," said Peter.

"What is this thing 'Love' anyway?" I asked in an exasperated tone, "I know all this is kind of corny. I don't even like the word. It even makes me feel uncomfortable to say it."

"I'm the same," said Steve in agreement.

"But it's true what they say. They sing about it, write about it in novels and magazines." They smiled and nodded.

"You hear it on TV, but when it comes to real life I've never seen or heard it in action. It's like a conspiracy of silence when you really want to know. Nobody can give you an understandable explanation."

"It's as though it's assumed," said Steve, "nobody questions it. Everybody assumes something is going to happen…..but what is it exactly?....and when?....and how?"

"For instance, when was the last time you saw a man and a woman meet each other, observe sparks flying, and then hear them say out loud, 'I love you.' and 'I love you, too.' clearly and lucidly, out in the open," Peter laughed.

"It doesn't happen like that," said Peter assuredly.

"Now suddenly Peter's the expert," observed Steve.

"How does it happen then?" I asked, "In dark corners, hidden away from view?"

"Sometimes," responded Peter.

"Doesn't sound like the best way to start a marriage? In a corner, hidden away," I suggested.

As we continued walking, the subject changed to more mundane matters concerning the flat, such as who was going to clean it up. It was a very short discussion. The possibility of marriage, however still lingered in my mind. This was my first real girlfriend. The relationship was good. This was beyond dispute. Perhaps there were sparks, perhaps this was love. Everyone observed we were made for each other. But now the expectations were shifting. More and more the innuendo was moving towards getting married. I was only twenty years old. Within this context the prospect of marrying seemed like a life sentence.

Perhaps I should have an affair with someone else without Jenna knowing. I had no desire to deliberately do that. Anyway, I wanted Jenna. I couldn't bear the thought of leaving Jenna and yet to experience another relationship could only destroy what we had. All this discussion with Peter about DNA and how it controlled behaviour surely ought to help. I now understood a lot of what controlled our feelings. But somehow it still didn't help. I was just as uncomfortable and feeling increasingly indecisive. Perhaps next year the problem would somehow resolve itself. Bury my head in the sand, just wait and see. Besides, surely it was more usual to marry when you leave college and have established yourself in work. Only at this time can you be in a position to buy a house and settle down. I wasn't really convincing myself of anything.

We were fast approaching the flat. Peter and Steve had started negotiating the cleaning rota again. I suddenly remembered my thoughts concerning DNA and realised that we had all been discussing this problem from our own point of view, a purely selfish act on our part, never a thought for the girls.

"Peter" I said interrupting, "I think you're right. Everything we seem to do is selfish."

"In Peter's case that's beyond dispute," confirmed Steve confidently.

CHAPTER FIVE

Time marched on ruthlessly. The years went so fast. I was visibly shocked to find myself with only days left before I would have to leave the university after my three-year BSc. and one-year MSc. It was as though I was refusing to accept it was going to end. I had settled so well into the daily patterns of college life, and in particular this college, that I had not prepared myself for leaving. That moment of realisation I will never forget. I simply didn't want to go. I had to say my goodbye's in a hurry. I would miss Peter, the Steve's, Toby, and Gary. Jenna and I had plans. No clear plans because I couldn't get a job. None of my applications were accepted, not one interview offered. I had nowhere to go. By a stroke of luck, however, the external examiner from Aston University in Birmingham had offered me a grant to do a Ph.D in Palynology. I didn't know what Palynology was at the time, but I agreed anyway. This was not the time to be choosy. I was now bound for Birmingham. College life was thus set to continue for another two years at least.

Preparation to enter Birmingham now introduced the purchase of an old minivan for 75 pounds. My long suffering, father had succumbed to putting windows in the rear so giving the very exclusive impression of an estate car. He had also resprayed it to a very original shade of brown and cream. The car was filled to the brim with clothes, blankets, books, my tape recorder and of course the guitar. This was to be a new adventure and I was now ready. The University had provided an address for digs and over the phone the arrangements had been confirmed. I set off without a care. For some strange reason I was not at all concerned about what lay ahead.

In those days it seemed a long journey from Rotherham to Birmingham. To join the A38, which took you direct from Derby, I had to pass through Mickleover which took me back to my early childhood. During the summer I always spent my school holidays with my sister who lived there. As I negotiated the traffic I looked over at the familiar streets and houses where I used to play at that time. I stared with horror at a new housing estate now smothering the green fields where I used to walk. I returned my attention to the road ahead. Unlike a few moments before, the way ahead now seemed cold and unfamiliar. To complete the atmosphere, it was now getting dark and it began to rain heavily. The rain rattled noisily on the car roof. Some of my earlier optimism was beginning to ebb. The flimsy, thin windscreen wipers that mini cars possessed were quite inadequate to cope with even the mildest of weather conditions. To add to the problems the engine temperature gauge was showing red; the engine was overheating. I was forced to stop. The radiator was empty. Fortunately, I was still close to civilisation so I walked over to the nearest house to ask for some water. An older lady came to the door. At first, she was very reluctant to give me any water. Instead she wanted to invite me in for a cup of tea and a sandwich. I explained again about the engine and she kindly obliged. Soon I was on my way again. It took two more stops to fill up the radiator before I was finally approaching Birmingham. The rain continued to pour. My nose was virtually glued to the windscreen as I furiously tried to rub away the condensation. I was heading for Moseley, but the road signs suggested otherwise.

When I finally did arrive, my engine was over heating and ready to explode. To my surprise the house where I was to stay appeared to be a very pleasant detached house. At least in the dim streetlights, it looked that way. I rushed to the front door, trying to avoid the rain. A rather pretty girl answered the door. She was petit and quite slim, with dark, densely curled hair wearing jeans with a maroon sweatshirt. She couldn't have been much older than myself. Not what I expected for a landlady.

"Yes…What do you want?" she said with difficulty. Her voice was just a little slurred.

"I spoke to you on the phone……about renting a room….I'm from the university," Her expression remained unchanged and rather blank. "I think you're expecting me?" I offered hopefully. Momentarily, her expression suggested recognition.

"Ah yes," she said, continuing to slur her words, "Come in, come in and I'll show you a good time…Oops!...I mean I will show you to your room… No, no , no, I won't …I'll introduce you to my husband first, and then you can take me to your room."

I followed her in through a short hallway into the living room. The room was lit only by candlelight. She pointed in a rather exaggerated manner towards three people sat together on the sofa. "The one in the middle is my husband Brian." She moved towards him and sat down, almost tumbling on to his lap. "And this is Pat and Victor, friends of ours," she said wrapping an arm around both of them, whilst leaning backwards, and almost suffocating her husband. Without appreciating her husband's predicament, she continued. "Everybody, this is Nick…….He's come to live with us."

"Ooh, he's nice," said Pat also with a slurred voice.

"Could I ask…I mean you didn't say your name?" I ventured, staring at my prospective landlady.

"And I'm Judy," she said proudly, and then changing to a very meek voice and putting an arm around her husband, giggled, "Did I forget me?"

"Yes, you did," giggled Pat.

"Look," I said apologetically, "I'm obviously interrupting your party. I can come back later. This was quite a magnanimous gesture of mine considering I had nowhere to go. Fortunately, it was ignored.

"No, of course not," said Brian finally. He groped his way free and stood up. He was not very tall and sported a substantial beard. "Just follow me."

"Oh no you don't…" said Judy. She slumped back into the sofa as she tried to get up. Brian led the way to one of the rooms upstairs only pausing briefly to show me the layout of things and then disappearing quickly back downstairs.

I switched on the light and sat on the bed. It was a nice room with the relative luxury of a curved Neo–Georgian bay window. This was, in fact, a double bedroom with what seemed acres of space. Everything seemed clean and fresh, and best of all, warm. Such a contrast to London. Outside the rain continued to pour down heavily. Despite this I decided to bring in a few of my belongings. The car was not entirely waterproof. After a few excursions I returned to sit on the bed. I looked around the room again. Downstairs the party clearly continued. I debated whether to find an excuse to go down again. The noise was becoming distinctly louder. I ventured downstairs. As I arrived at the glass paned lounge door, I could make out the vague outline of people dancing.

"It's time to ask for a glass of something," I thought to myself, "after all it has been a long drive." I knocked on the door and waited. Nothing. It was futile for me to expect them to hear anything with the noise. I banged on the door again, very loud this time and stepped in, "Sorry for the intrusion but I wondered if I might have…" I stopped. Without a hint of embarrassment, the four of them were dancing topless. I finished the sentence, "…a glass of milk?" But they didn't hear. Although I had never taken drugs, I had the distinct impression that this joyous atmosphere had been helped along by something other than alcohol.

"Hi!" waved Judy. Her breasts were being fully displayed to me, her large dark nipples conspicuous, swaying to and fro as she tried to dance.

"Come in," said Pat, "take your shirt off."

For some unforgivable reason I just couldn't. I was stone cold sober and although quite excited by the sight, found myself retreating. I was just not conversant in these ways. I was taken too much by surprise. "It's ok," I said embarrassingly, "just carry on…" Then before I knew it, I was sat back on the bed again, visibly trembling from the scenes I had just witnessed. I stared over at the rain pounding on the big, bay window. "What a waste!" I grumbled to myself.

The next day I went directly to the university without breakfast (to save embarrassment) and to meet my new supervisor, Dr. Mavis Butterworth. We had met only once before. I drove in via the Bull Ring, a labyrinth of motorway and tunnels ringing the heart of the city and parked in a side street close by. I looked up at the main building as it towered upwards forming a dark foreboding silhouette against the bright sky. The windows and walls had a somber, almost prison like appearance. I walked along the side, which was cold, hidden from the sun, and in the dark shadow it cast, only to be dazzled as I turned a corner. The entrance was on a far larger scale than the college in London. I asked for directions at the rather grandiose, but old fashioned, reception. The hall was marble lined and was distinguished by having a very high cathedral like ceiling. The echoey sound of shuffling feet and the low hum of chattering voices emphasised the church atmosphere. I had to go up to the seventh floor and so moved towards the lift area. I was a little off put by the absence of any kind of door on the lifts. Even more off putting, however, was that the lifts appeared never to stop and one was supposed to hop into one of the constantly rotating cubicles and then hop out again as required. I stood and watched momentarily before venturing. They seemed to be travelling quite fast. The experience turned out to be quite fun and I arrived safe and sound, one floor above where I was supposed to be. I took the stairway back down. The corridor led me to where the Geology Department was supposed to be. I looked around at the bare walls and stared into a single lecture room. There was no one around to ask so I wandered over to a door on the other side of the lecture room. This led to another short corridor which had a bench and some equipment squeezed into it. There was one more door to try. As I opened it I was hit by the overpowering stale smell of tobacco and then saw someone sitting at a desk.

"Oops, sorry, I'm looking for the Geology Department." I said trying to excuse myself and get back into the fresh air. An older lady with grey hair and a portly appearance sat puffing heavily on her cigarette.

"Yes, that's here." She said, and as she spoke I recognised it was Mavis. She smiled as she took another puff on her cigarette and then asked, "Are you looking for somebody in particular?"

"Well actually, I think I'm looking for you." I said boldly, "Dr. Butterworth?"

"Are you Nick Townsend?" I nodded. "We were expecting you to come last week."

My heart sank. "A week late....Oh no!" I thought.

"Did you have some trouble with the traffic?" she mused. "It's no bother, we were just beginning to wonder," she said still clasping her cigarette to her mouth.

Her response was quite friendly. In fact, there was a jovial ring to her voice and possibly the smallest indication of a twinkle in her eye as she spoke. Mavis was a highly respected scientist in her field and was world renowned. Some of her work was the basis for all present thinking and developments within the subject. I felt quite in awe of her achievements. Yet she presented herself as a very kindly person but yet not without wit and a clear perspective.

After a short and very informal discussion she offered to show me my working area. I was aghast to discover it was to be the little corridor. No windows, no privacy. It would most likely be a walkway for many. I was very disappointed to think I was to spend possibly the next three years just here. I tried not to show my disappointment. But I think I did. We returned to her room and then out again through a second door into a large open area with desks.

"I'll introduce you to the others," she said looking around for someone. A single student sat at a desk. He was slim built, with black hair and a neatly trimmed beard. He looked a few years older than myself. "This is Stuart Reeves, he has just started working, and on a similar a project to yourself. Perhaps you could take over now and show Nick the rest of the place."

Stuart and I went to find a cup of coffee which was to be found on the top floor. We negotiated the novel lift system and entered the large coffee lounge. Finding a space we sat down. I stared at him briefly trying to assess his manner.

"Which university did you come from…that is, where did you get your first degree?" I began.

"Right here in Birmingham," he replied, "I decided to become a teacher first but then decided to go on for more qualifications."

"You must really like children then…to do teaching?" I asked impertinently.

"I like girls," he said pointedly and left the words hanging in the air. I didn't pursue the matter further.

"So, you must be fairly familiar with this place."

"In a way, but being married I usually return home rather than involve myself in university life……What do you think of Mavis?"

"Smokes too much, I suspect." From his expression he didn't like my tone.

"She's a good sport," he responded, rallying to her defence. "What's your field area?"

"The Carboniferous ….of Ireland."

"Ooo ah mi hearties, shiver mi timbers……" he began spontaneously putting on the voice of Long John Silver and then almost immediately realising this had nothing to do with Ireland switched to a sort of Irish accent, "……No, no that's completely wrong, I mean bijabes, bijabes , bijabes and the top of the mornin' to you!"

Now this outburst may not retell as very amusing, but the manner in which he said it, was actually very funny and made me laugh. He was making an effort to be friendly, and I appreciated that.

"Take no notice of me," trying to recover himself.

"Do you have a name for that merry go round of a lift system?" I asked curiously.

"Oh that thing…Have you tried it yet?" he said vaguely turning in their direction.

"Yes I tried it …It's like stepping on to a bacon slicer."

"It's called a Paternoster, but don't ask me why."

"It's probably Italian for bacon slicer……I wonder how they stand with the insurance?" I mused.

"You mean if someone gets mangled? I wonder if they've even thought about it," said Stuart thoughtfully.

On our return to the department I found a letter waiting for me. It was from Jenna. As I read it the content began to startle me a little. The innuendoes with regard to marriage were increasing and she was clearly feeling the change in our circumstances. With me being in Birmingham and her in Chesterfield it seemed our situation was on hold. Despite being provided with an opportunity to make a break, all I could feel at this moment was the need to find a telephone and to just talk with her. To hear her voice again. Stuart had watched me read the letter and waited for me as I folded it up and placed it carefully into my pocket.

"Are you married?" he enquired.

"No, the letter was from my girlfriend."

"I am!" he stated proudly. The words were clearly emphasized. "Actually, why don't you come round one evening this weekend and meet the wife." Something suddenly took his attention and amused him. He tried to smother a smile. "You know," he began thoughtfully, "The one thing I really like about girls are boobs. So long as they have boobs, I'm hooked." The statement was brutal but intended. It had an almost classical fundamentalism about it as he paused to acknowledge this simple truth.

After completing this statement he relaxed slightly, as though some sudden surge of wind had been successfully negotiated, and had now subsided. I answered his invitation. His eyes previously glazed, now focused again. "Ah yes….sorry….what was that? Yes let's do that. I'll draw you a map."

During the week I met the other postgraduates, and several of the staff. It was clear, however, that I most easily got along with Stuart. His mildly impish humour appealed to me.

I also discovered the whereabouts of another friend. A piano stood that in the main hall of the student's union. So long as there were no functions, it was free to be played. To my delight I managed to develop, within a relatively short time, three new melodies and then proceeded to use much of the remaining week recording piano tracks.

When the music flows it's like a karma. The feeling of rhythm and melody is so pleasant you don't want to stop. In such a state it's not unusual to play for an hour, or even two, without pausing. This was "drugs" without drugs, an addiction. Afterwards, however, it feels like a dreadful waste. I had definitely used far too much time on this particular project. Somehow, I would have to make this time up. To ease my guilty conscience, I worked on my rock sampling program for several late nights.

As arranged, on the Saturday I made my way to the south of Birmingham to visit Stuart at his home. Surprisingly, he had a large detached modern house set in a quiet rural area; distinctly affluent for a student like me. I suddenly felt untidy in my usual jeans and pullover. I knocked on the glass-paneled door. The cool wind of winter blew around me as I waited. The door opened.

"Ah, come in, come in," said Stuart with a jolly voice, "meet the wife!"

As we stepped into the large living room I was struck by the neat and tidy layout. Everything was well organised and in its place. As a student such sights were rare. His wife Beth got up out of her chair to greet me. She was vivacious and shapely and Stuart noticeably displayed her as though she was a prize to be admired. The visit went well. We began dinner and drank a lot. It became apparent that Stuart was also very interested in music and played the drums. The conversation at first leaned heavily towards musicians and musical trivia of all kinds. Unfortunately, his interest was in the area of jazz which was not my first choice. Undaunted by this, we arranged a visit to the famous Gas Street Jazz Club to hear the real thing. I felt honoured by the invitation and was really beginning to enjoy the friendship. Beth, I could see, had heard enough about jazz.

"What's your area of interest, Beth?" I asked curiously.

"I teach science, but I'm quite interested in classical philosophy."

"That's a great combination," I said, trying to catch her attention. "You're in a good position to provide some answers."

"Well, I don't know about that. But I do like Classical Philosophers," a little puzzled by my comment.

"I'm not so sure about them," I said, a little disappointed.

"How can you say that? Have you studied them in that much detail?" she asked looking a little annoyed.

"Not really. It's just from what I've heard. All questions and no answers," It was my genuine impression from the many discussions I had endured with my older sister who had a passion for Philosophy.

"This is abrasive stuff Nicholas," she almost shouted. "But I suspect you don't know what you are talking about." This last comment was said with more feeling, her eyes more tense. I took a sip of wine.

"I'm sure you're right of course." I said sort of apologetically. It was a little presumptuous of me. After all I barely knew Beth. Beth looked across to Stuart and smiled. She didn't look at all irritated and got up to get a bottle of wine from a cupboard. She looked elegant as she moved across the room. It really caught my attention. Then as she sat, she gave me just the faintest smile.
"All I mean is that philosophers ask the questions, but it is science that answers them." I was trying to adopt a more studious tone. "Let me put it this way. Any philosophical,

point, conundrum, call it what you will, that you may put to me, I can probably answer with a reasonable scientific explanation. And it shouldn't be "Will England ever win the World Cup again?" I said boldly.

"Ah ha…so you can't answer everything!" said Stuart jumping in.

"Perhaps you're right!" I said with a shocked expression.

"Come on Beth think of something," I followed, urging her on. She didn't really look that keen to carry on with this.

"I don't know," she said full of hesitation, "I can't think of anything specific right now. The wine has fuzzed up my head."

"I only want to challenge your philosophers," I said wanting her to continue. "You never know I might learn something."

"Ok I'll be boring and suggest something. Most philosophical questions centre around such things as; What is truth?…What is morality?..etc…Until eventually the ultimate…What is the meaning of life?….Which everyone knows is the number 42." I paused but didn't wait for the obvious reaction, "but I think I can answer all questions employing one universal principle."

"Go on then," said Stuart drolly, "what's the punch line? Pull the rabbit out of the hat."

I paused. I knew what I was about to say can sound banal and can bring conversations to an embarrassing halt.

"The answer lies in …..the Alien Within Us."

It was supposed to be a moment of great impact, a new dawn of understanding. Instead I had said it far too glibly. I just didn't get the right effect I was hoping for. For a moment there was silence. Then Beth began to laugh.

"Come on Nick, what is this so called universal principle? What's the punch-line?" said Stuart not at all impressed.

"I told you … The Alien Within," I replied with a mild tone of insistence. "It's not supposed to be comical. I actually think it's a little frightening….sort of eerie."

"You mean Von Daniken and the space invaders?" he asked.

"No, not at all, that's quite another story," I replied emphatically. I picked up my wine to take a sip. Beth picked up the bottle and poured more wine into the glass. As she leaned over I became suddenly aware her blouse was not only unbuttoned but in certain directions quite see-through. I looked up at Beth in time to see that she had observed me looking. I felt caught out; embarrassed and quickly tried to glance away. She stared at me knowingly as I tried to recover myself. Despite my best efforts I sounded embarrassed. Undaunted I continued. They sat back to listen.

"The alien gremlins came from galaxies billions of light years away, dispersed by comets travelling the cosmos, looking for a new home. They found it when they crash landed on the newly formed Earth's crust over half a billion years ago." The way I was saying this sounded grandiose, not my usual style but I continued. I was enjoying the moment.

"They landed as minute organic particles preserved in ice and possessing a copying code able to reproduce and sustain themselves when provided with a suitable environment and building material. Here on Earth they had all the right ingredients. All Earthbound attempts at trying to build sustainable organic molecular structures had failed. The alien visitors began in earnest building structure after structure. They had the unique ability to build organic hosts that would nurture and protect them. Even better, their hosts, if damaged or decaying had the ability to regenerate themselves over and over again, each time developing more advanced and sophisticated protective devices and survival skills until finally today they are even able to discuss the matter with other fellow hosts, introspectively, over dinner." I slowed down over this latter part hoping they would notice the irony.

I stopped for a moment to see their reaction. They were both sat pensively leaning over the table; their eyes still staring at me, waiting for more.

"I presume the alien you are talking about is DNA," said Stuart.

I smiled.

"How does this explain morality and truth?" asked Beth.

"I'm glad you asked me that." I said trying desperately to concentrate my focus only on Beth's face and nowhere else. "The only truth is the continuation of the alien, which is the DNA. We must be true to this and nothing else. If we ever carry out any action that threatens this situation then it hits us with pain, doubt, guilt and remorse. If we pursue our only true course correctly, it rewards us with pleasure and happiness. But only for a fleeting moment." I emphasised. "It wants us to remain vigilant and attentive at all times; to maximise our, and subsequently their, survival. As a result, most of our lives are spent performing survival strategies for those morsels of happiness and pleasure that will ensure both our, and their, existence now and in the future. Morality is merely the code of behaviour required to nurture their existence and continuation…..Eerie isn't it. We are just the hosts to an alien life force."

They continued to sit and stare without comment.

"I think it's eerie," I said again trying to extract comment. I was beginning to miss Peter.

"Are you going to write it down?" asked Stuart.

"I hadn't thought about doing that. I'm enjoying just playing with the concepts," I replied. In fact, I had thought about it but the truth was I was frightened. My writing abilities were poor. In reality, I had never read a book about philosophy, psychology or any of these subjects. If I tried to write this down, I felt sure that those who were studying this subject seriously would have shot it down in flames.

"But isn't the host and the alien one and the same thing?" asked Beth pertinently.

"I believe the DNA can be viewed as some sort of seed….A life force" I suggested. "It could build anything…giant orange blobs on one galaxy, wardrobes on another….anything." I mused, and then continued. "Pieces of amino acids remnant from previous alien life cycles, possibly from many different parts of the cosmos, that had evolved and were then destroyed, casualties always of an explosive and violent universe. These tiny fertile molecular structures could survive and over a colossal time scale. They eventually accumulated as a part of the cosmic dust ready to shower down on an unsuspecting new planet. It's no different to the reproduction mechanisms employed by tiny organisms in the great oceans here on Earth. It makes us just one more micro-life cycle within a vast limitless recycling of the organic dust."

"But what's the purpose to all this?" asked Stuart sounding a little bereft.

"There is nothing magical. Just a life force building and constructing, building and constructing…..just like the tides of the seas go in and out ….An apparent mindless repetitive cycle." I said sadly. "We have been sent a little map which we must follow religiously. We are obliged to do this, without choice, hooked by the morsels of pleasure, if we do, and the fear of pain, if we don't." I hesitated briefly.

"The thought of this mindless repetition is so depressing." I said slightly raising my tone. "But we cannot kick the habit. Life is an addiction."

"Are you really depressed?" asked Beth sympathetically.

"Nah….course not. I just like a good story." I said suddenly springing to life. "I like the thoughts of us all being addicts though. It's really warped…an alien force that constructs its host to be addictive to itself….that's got to be a mind bender. "

"So, what are you going to do with this new found knowledge?" asked Beth, "If you say it's so mindless."

"Nothing I suppose….It isn't the magic cure I was hoping to discover, that's for sure." I said enigmatically. "I think it helps me understand my own feelings and desires etc, especially desires!" said emphatically.

"Oh yes?" responded Beth with a glint in her eye.

"Yes." I said with a knowing smile. "But what I'm really thinking is that it helps to rationalise your own peculiar selfish desires and why you have them and why other people have their different desires. It frees me from the childish religious guilt that is imposed. It also helps me make decisions. We are all merely trying to follow the little map we've been given inside us. All of them very similar but each of them different."

"But haven't philosophers always said this? We're all the same but different?" suggested Beth again attempting to minimalise the statement.

"Exactly, but they never explained it. They never understood it."

Beth stood up to pour out more wine. This time, as she leaned over, a large area of her cleavage was clearly exposed for me to see. I found myself staring directly into her blouse.

"Beautiful, aren't they?" said Stuart observing my gaze. "My total obsession in life. They make you want to reach in and devour them." He seemed to be inviting me to do so.

"Too much wine Stuart," I said trying to deflect further comment. The incident passed but I was left to ponder the moment. Despite my cosmic visions, such liberal thoughts shocked me. It wasn't long, however, before his conversation returned again to his wife's open blouse, this time accompanied by some details of their sexual exploits in the bedroom. He wasn't being literally direct, but the innuendo was becoming more and more racy. I tried my best not to react. Maybe it was just a word game. I had never really been involved in conversations like this. Beth didn't react at all, allowing him his suggestions and even acknowledging his appreciating remarks. However, it did seem to be leading in one direction. Suddenly the phone rang. Stuart got up to answer it.

"I'm afraid a neighbour of ours has got into a bit of bother. Unfortunately, I'll have to go and help him out," he said disappointedly. "It looks like I'll be a while. Why don't you stay and chat to Beth."

An opportunity was staring me in the face, but I made my excuses and decided it was an appropriate time to leave.

The journey home was filled with frustration. The temperature in the car was warm and my mind bedraggled with alcohol and the fleeting glimpses of Beth's open blouse. My mind wrestled to calm itself. Stuart and Beth were open to suggestion. I even suspected that Stuart had pre-empted the incidents so that events might have developed. All of this was, of course exciting, but I reminded myself of the morning after. What kind of a morning would that have been? I decided that by doing absolutely nothing, I had in fact taken the right course of action. I still didn't feel any better about anything.

By now I was approaching the centre of Birmingham. The lights of the city were subdued. It was quite late, twelve o'clock. I passed the Cobra Discotheque where the lights were brighter and there was the suggestion of continuing nightlife. As if possessed, the car steered itself into the carpark and into the nearest parking slot. I stepped out of the car and began to sense the lateness of the hour. I also began to sense the state of my appearance. My shirt, pullover and trousers were distinctly drab. There was nothing I could do about that. What a contrast, I suddenly thought, one minute discussing the Universe in all its glory;

the next minute furtively scouring a night club for who knows what.

The throbbing beat of the music rang out into the midnight air of the carpark like a church bell beckoning. I walked up to the ticket office.

"How much is it?" I politely asked.

"Ten shillings!" she said abruptly as if, somehow, everyone should know. She took the money without expression. I strolled into the room and let the rhythm of the music bathe over me; like entering a shower before swimming.

"Excuse me sir!" exclaimed a gruff voice firmly, "could you step this way for a moment."

I tried to think of which sacred law I had managed to transgress already.

"Are you wearing jeans?" he demanded. As he looked me up and down I didn't answer. "We don't allow blue jeans in here sir." He was brusk but reluctantly he gave me the all clear. Undaunted I moved towards the bar. The dance floor occupied the centre of the room and was surrounded by a mock tropical setting dominated by plastic palm trees. I obtained a pint of beer. It tasted warm and watery. A band played love songs evocatively. In the gloom the on looking males were finally moving in to take their various partners, claimed by the ritual stares and glances during earlier stages of the evening. I'd obviously arrived at the right time; avoiding all the earlier stages. Although in retrospect, these times usually transpired to be the right time for somebody else, never me. I sipped the warm beer and glanced around at the few available girls dancing alone. Only a few groups left. I began to have second thoughts about all this. I was on my own and I felt conspicuous as though I shouldn't be there on my own. Without drinking the beer I turned to go.

"Don't go yet," said a voice. A pretty but very small young lady passed by me on her way back to the dance floor. Despite her angelic features and sylphlike figure she stood only five and a bit, feet tall. The top of her head barely met with my chest. I followed her onto the dance floor.

"I thought you were going?" she enquired and continued to carve a way through the endless bobbing sea of dancers. I continued to follow. Finally, she stopped. In stark contrast, she began dancing with an equally pretty but very tall young lady.

"I was just about to go," I said and began dancing.

"You looked lonely," she shouted, the words being quickly lost in amongst the noise of the music. I smiled, looked around the dance floor and continued dancing. "This is Susan," she said introducing the tall girl. "And I'm Jackie." I nodded in acknowledgement.

"Nick!" I shouted, pointing to myself. My eyes glanced around the room, trying hard not to stare from the tall one to the small one. "It's no good," I thought to myself, "neither of them are the right size." I leaned down, what seemed a long way, to speak to Jackie. "I'll have to be going soon." She nodded.

"Could you give us a lift?"

"If you live in Moseley, I can,"

"We live in Edgebaston." she said hopefully. With that they both bent down to pick up their handbags and again I found myself following through the crowded dance floor as they both made their way purposely towards the exit. Outside the rain had held off.

"Where's your car?" they enquired in unison.
"Car?" I replied with feigned surprise. "What car?" I said firmly, "I have a tandem." They paused, pulling their coats on tighter; the tall one looking down and small one looking up to see if I was joking. "Come on, it's not a tandem."

"Oh what a pity," they announced disappointedly. Susan and Jackie shuffled into the back seat and I sat in the front like a regular taxi driver.

"Where to ladies?"

I looked in my rear view mirror. All I could see was Susan's shoulders and the top of Jackie's head.

"Remember, out of town and after midnight can turn out quite expensive."

"We've spent all our money," said Jackie, "On fellas."

"And I haven't got any," added Susan quickly.

"Okay, for two pretty ladies like yourselves, the management reserves the right to make a special courtesy free offer," said jokingly.

"Well, thankyou kind sir," said Jackie "in that case we accept."

We drove off into the night and eventually arrived, somewhere in the midst of Edgebaston, where they shared a flat. All the streets in this area looked very much alike and I had turned so many corners that I really had no idea where I was. We pulled to a halt and they asked me in for a coffee. I followed them up a narrow stairway up to the first floor above a shop. Their flat comprised a large room with a kitchen area screened off. Jackie sat down on one of the two single beds which served as sofas, whilst Susan disappeared into the kitchen area. Out of curiosity, I looked into the kitchen. Susan was busy with the coffee. She had long dark hair and easily stood a few inches taller than myself.

"So, you're the cook in the house?" I asked weakly trying to make conversation.

"Not always, we usually share," she replied and with that she reached out and pulled lightly on my arm and gave me a kiss. I was surprised, especially since, I assumed I was with Jackie; although it all seemed a little premature at this stage. I returned the kiss. There was a slight pause and then she continued making the coffee. I used this moment to return to Jackie. As I sat down, Jackie virtually repeated the procedure, taking my arm and pulling me gently towards her. Susan sat herself at the other side of me. Despite the obvious attraction of this situation, the alcoholic influence was beginning to fade, and I just sat there feeling uncomfortable. I began to think about the letter Jenna had just sent. She had asked so many questions in this letter that I couldn't now stop them coming into my mind.

"You are going to marry me," she had written, "I couldn't bear it if you didn't."

I looked from side to side at Susan and Jackie. "It's no good," I thought, "I just can't continue with this….Size does matter." At an appropriate moment I decided to make my excuses for the second time this evening and left. They were not very pleased.

I stepped out into the cold night air and looked soulfully up at the dim starlight in the black sky. Looking back down I suddenly became aware that my car wasn't where I expected it to be. I looked again and then again, as though by some miracle these moments might be erased before they became too entrenched in reality. Alas reality prevailed. The car had definitely gone, vanished, disappeared.

Not having been in this situation before I pondered the options. The police had to be informed; so, I should telephone as soon as possible. Do I walk home, or should I ask for shelter in the arms of the two young ladies upstairs? I could telephone the police at the same time. What could be more natural? They were quite attractive. For a few moments I visualised the possibilities. Something else, however, told me I would just be an embarrassment. I had one more look up the stairway and then turned to walk down the street in the direction of home. I fastened my coat and shoved my hands deep into my pockets to keep warm. I could feel the crumpled shape of an envelope and realised I still had Jenna's letter. I straightened it out and read it as I walked along.

The next day I managed to retrieve the car. It had already been found by the police abandoned at the other side of Birmingham and they had impounded it in their giant caged carpark for lost and unwanted cars. Fortunately, it wasn't damaged. The only evidence of it being stolen were two wires left dangling from behind the dashboard, which had been used to start the engine. More important that day was the arrival of another letter from Jenna. It confirmed that she had been awarded a place at the polytechnic, an M.Sc. course in Town Planning and would be able to start in the new term. I decided almost immediately to look for another bedsit or flat for both of us. I rang Jenna to let her know.

"I received your letter." I began in a controlled voice.

"It's good news, isn't it?" She always had an attractive tone to her voice. I liked it and was glad to hear it again. "I didn't really believe I would get a place so near the beginning of term."

"Where will you be staying?" dodging the question.

"Do you think it would be easy to find a bedsit near your side of Birmingham?"

"It's easy to find a hovel," I said drolly.

"I'm not interested in a hovel," she retorted sternly.

"I'll do my best to find something suitable."

"You'll do better than that. I'm coming down to help you."

I felt the reality of decision time encroaching. I wanted to immediately say "Lets live together," with a warm hearted feeling of enthusiasm, but her abrupt response was getting in the way. I held back and said nothing.

"I said I will be coming down to help you," interrupted Jenna's voice.

Why did it sound like a threat? I asked myself. "That's great!" trying to sound enthusiastic.

"You don't want me to come....Do you?" she asked plaintively.

"Of course I do," trying to recover the situation.

"Look, I'm sorry if I'm intruding into your life," she said

again plaintively.

"That's not true. In fact, I was going to suggest we look for a place to share," I said defensively.

"Are you really?" she asked with a sense of relief.

"Yes." I replied firmly.

"You mean you want us to live together?" she continued, now with an almost girlish, voice. "Does that mean we will..." She didn't finish the sentence. I rapidly searched for a change of course.

"When will you be coming down?" I said quickly.

"This Saturday, early morning, will you meet me?"

Within a few short weeks all the arrangements had been completed. The flat was located at the end of a, not so attractive, red brick row of terraced houses in Edgebaston. It was a first floor flat with its own entrance and stairway. Basically, it had two rooms and a shared bathroom. At this stage no one occupied the adjacent flat, so we were relatively private. Jenna had no illusions about the place. Apparently the colour scheme was offensive and had to be changed immediately, which we did. A new activity entered my everyday life called shopping. We shopped for paints, for furniture, for kitchen utensils and for food. Despite the initial feeling of actually being dragged around the shops, I eventually grew into it a little. It seemed to bring us together a little more. I wasn't given a chance to settle until the place had a new face and a new fresh smell about it. Other things had changed. My thinking time was re-arranged. The drive to college was usually a very quiet affair, a time for thoughts to roam. Not any more, today the drive to college was quite different.

Jenna took my arm as I closed the door to the front of the flat. As she made her way purposely around the other side of the car, she paused to smile at me before entering. She looked very attractive. I settled down in the driver's seat. The car started first time, which was a relief. At first my thoughts began to drift off into the usual areas of musical construction, trying to complete melodic phrases left incomplete the previous day.

"I'd like to invite Robert and Nina this weekend, if I may," began Jenna, "would you mind if I did that?"

"No, not at all," I replied, not really giving it any thought. Robert and Nina were friends of Jenna's from schooldays who now apparently, lived in the Birmingham area. There was still a melodic phrasing in my mind which I was still trying to hang on to before it faded and disappeared. The main theme repeated itself and I was becoming self-hypnotised by the various attempts to finish the tune. It was almost there. I could sense it.

"Are you going to finish the dining room table so that we can seat everybody?" asked Jenna enthusiastically.

"What?" I murmured, still locked in another world.

"The table just needs that extra coat of varnish" she continued, "shall we go together this lunchtime to buy some more varnish?" Her tone was enthusiastic.

"Yes, I suppose so," I replied.

"Where shall we meet?" asked Jenna.

We were on the Birmingham ring road and I was trying to juggle my musical thoughts with the encroaching traffic, as well as listen to the essentials of what Jenna was saying.

"What?" I grunted vaguely.

My replies were becoming shorter. I realised this and decided to make a more concentrated effort to please.

"Oh yes," I quickly added, "Let's meet somewhere for lunch....Any ideas?"

"Not at all," responded Jenna, surprised I should be asking, "this is my first day at college!"

"Sorry, I was forgetting," I said apologetically. "I suppose you're looking forward to this morning then?"

I indicated left and turned off to park the car down a side road along quite close to college.

"I'm not really looking forward to this at all," she followed. "I hate academics......It's not what I want to do." The tone of her voice lowered as she turned her head to face forward, deliberately away from a view of the college. "You know I'm here only for you." She turned to face me, looking worried. I knew what she wanted me to say, and I wanted too. I really wanted too. But I couldn't, not then.

We walked the rest of the way to college together. I put my arm around her and tried to squeeze her. I wanted her to feel happier. She stopped and reached up to kiss me. It felt good. We made our arrangements to meet for lunch and then watched her walk across the large barren area that lay before the Polytechnic's entrance. The polytechnic was a modern building of the sixties, functional at best but a slum already, and depressing in reality. Large concrete walls surrounded by deserts of windswept paving stones. Her pace quickened, her head lowered as she clutched her books tight to her chest. I took a curious pleasure in watching her as she finally reached the main doorway and disappeared.

My thoughts were suddenly wrenched into reality as glimpses of the college work ahead of me entered finally into my head. This term would be difficult. To be more positive I should say it would be challenging. The field work I had completed last year had proved only partly successful. It required another trip to Ireland, and all of this needed to be organised. Meanwhile I was struggling along with the limited materials I had. As I entered the department, I immediately noticed that several of the desks had been re-arranged. Formerly I had my microscope on a bench situated in the corridor. Now, it appeared, I had a desk within the main research room back to back with Stuart.

"Aha!" exclaimed Stuart as I walked in.

"Aha," I replied in similar vain as I took in some the changes. "Uhuh." I continued, more or less, approving what I saw.

"Uhuh." followed Stuart as he also stared in an obvious way around the room.

"Hmph!" I snorted as I laid down my brief case heavily on the floor.

"A desk is certainly a novelty," I continued. "Pity about the view." Realising I would be staring straight across at Stuart. "Perhaps if you could wear a little lipstick?"

"But I do!" he said with cheesy grin.

"So how was your vacation?" enquired Stuart.

"It started normally but finished rather unexpectedly," I

replied, "how was yours?"

"What do you mean unexpected?" his curiosity raised.

"Well, I bought a new toothbrush," I said jokingly.

"About time," he quipped.

"Ok, I've moved into a flat with Jenna," I said and waited for the reaction.

"You've got married!"

"No, no," I interrupted. "No." I said again. "Jenna got herself a place in the Town Planning M.Sc. course, here in Birmingham." I paused, "and so we decided to live together."

"That's great," said Stuart with a genuine enthusiasm, "isn't it? Is this a secret?"

"I'm not sure," I pondered vaguely. I hadn't actually thought about the consequences of going public.

"Why don't you get married?" he asked insistently.

"I'm not sure," I said again.

"You've talked of no-one else," he followed. "When do I get to meet her?"

"Soon enough, no doubt." I began to investigate my new desk.

The following days went quickly. We entertained Robert and Nina, which was soon followed by a night out with Stuart and Beth, including a fantastic night out at the Gas

Street Club, a major jazz venue. Despite these social activities, I enjoyed the evenings at home in the flat, most of all. Just Jenna and myself. Jenna would often busy herself with making clothes, something she was very adept at. Her favorite was a large bedspread made up from a tapestry of small patterned squares taken from all sorts of different but similarly coloured materials which she sewed together. It took up most of her time. Such evenings were an opportunity for me to record pieces of music and songs; an activity not always welcomed.

"I'd like to buy an electric keyboard," I announced suddenly one evening as we sat down together. "You know, the type that are touch sensitive, that I've described before. They sound more like a real piano than the others," I added enthusiastically. Jenna looked up from her sewing and smiled weakly.

"It's trying to find the right one," I continued.

"Are they expensive," enquired Jenna.

"Some are, but I'm only looking out for the basic model."

"You should be saving your money really," suggested Jenna.

"What do you mean by that?" I asked, wondering what to expect.
"Shouldn't we be starting a building society account."

"What for?" I asked naively. I was walking headlong into trouble.

"So, we can save up for a house of our own," came the quiet reply.

I didn't answer and as a consequence there was a noticeable and uncomfortable pause. The pause developed into a silence and before I knew it, I had picked up my guitar and was strumming a few chords. Jenna shuffled her position, put down her sewing and went into the kitchen. I put down the guitar and used the space to try and relax from the building tension. After a few moments Jenna strode back into the room.

"Why don't you say anything!" she exclaimed with a tremor in her voice.

"About?" I said obviously.

"About us!" she shouted. "Why won't you bloody well say something?"

She was right, of course. I kept all the positive thoughts to myself. It was a defense mechanism.

"I'm twenty two years old, with virtually no experience and not yet working." I said, trying to find some words. "There's a big world out there with lots of options, hundreds of them that neither of us have had chance to consider yet. Here we are living together virtually isolating ourselves from this big open book in front of us." "Do you want to deny yourself all this?"

"You want me to go, don't you." she said in tearful surprise. My heart melted to see her cry. That's not what I meant at all. Actually I didn't know what I meant.

"No, I don't want you to go....Of course I don't want you to go." I went over to her and held her close. I could feel the wetness on her cheek as I attempted to kiss her. I felt awful that I could to be doing this to her. There just seemed no escape. She felt soft and warm. I felt for the first time that I wanted her and nobody else. Coincidently from downstairs, in the flat below, we could hear the sound of muffled shouting. It was a row and a very heated row. We pulled away from each other and listened. The sound of objects being thrown was conspicuous. It seemed an embarrassing coincidence and it made us smile at each other. The noise stopped.

"Let's go to bed," suggested Jenna. The moment had passed, and any problems postponed for another day.

The next day I continued my pursuit for an electric piano. I searched the magazines and found a small 'ad' that interested me. It was in Sheffield, so we used the excuse to return home. I found my way to the address. It was a semi-detached house perched characteristically on one of the many hills to the edge of Sheffield. Despite the city's industrial past these hills made a grandiose and dramatic impact on the scenery. A feature, I became more and more aware of being away in London and Birmingham. I liked it. I thought it was beautiful.

The owner of the piano was a tall, fair-haired guy, close to my age and very interested in the same kinds of music. Despite the piano turning out to be not quite what I was hoping for he invited me to play in his newly formed band. I had no serious expectations, but I was excited at the prospect of just being a part of something musical. Ideas almost immediately flooded into my head. Songs, their arrangements, it was something I had to do.

I drove over to Jenna's parents' house that evening, where I had been invited to dinner. Relations with her parents remained at a cool level and the occasion passed with a sense of relief. The journey back to Birmingham was spent explaining why I needed to go through with this musical exercise. We didn't argue. I think Jenna realised it was a futile exercise and at some stage inevitable. Nevertheless, her reaction was measured and balanced and I sensed the need to appease. My small mini-van made its way hesitantly along the A56, a poorly lit road at night and with a great amount of concentrated effort. I kept my eyes fixed on the wandering centre line in the road. It felt a little like one of those games found in amusement arcades. Occasionally, oncoming cars would dazzle with their piercing headlights. Illuminated by the lights I could observe the attractive profile of Jenna's face as she stared with equal intensity at the road ahead. She turned to look at me with her large dark brown eyes and then without speaking looked back at the road. I returned to look at her several times, each time her eyes speaking softly back to me. No words were necessary. Despite our previous discussions it seemed as if we were at peace with each other.

"Maybe this is the time to ask her?" I thought inwardly. 'Will you marry me? Let's get married' But I didn't. The moment passed as I remained attentive to the road.

The following day was a Sunday and we walked together around the park at Edgebaston. We discussed our respective families; pointed fingers at their so called, faults and reminisced about old friends. Back at the flat Jenna prepared an essay for college and I began to experiment with ideas for the prospective band.

"When will you be going to Ireland?" she asked, bringing me back to reality. I'd quite forgotten how imminent this trip was. I had only six months left before my research period was terminated. In this period, I had to obtain sufficient sample material in order to establish a viable database.

"You're right, I have to prepare myself very soon."

"How long will you have to take?" she asked again. It took me a month last time, but this time I realised it would be less.

"Just over a week, I think." I answered, quickly putting together a few thoughts about the arrangements. "Why, will you miss me?"

"Of course I will," she said, almost embarrassed, "I was just wondering that's all. I don't know everything you do."

The following morning, I was still planning the trip, I unexpectedly received a letter from London. It was from a musical agent that had shown some interest in the songs I'd sent.

Dear Nick,

We liked your songs and played them to Colin Blunstone. He is planning to record a new single very shortly and wishes to use one of your songs called "If you really don't know". Could you contact me with a view to making a demo-recording of this and two of the other songs, as soon as possible?

Yours,
Brian Reid.

Quickly I read over the content of the letter again. I couldn't believe it. I read it again and again, my eyes moistening with excitement. What joy this gave. A dream come true. To think of a professional recording made of my song. I ran back up the stairs to tell Jenna. She was less than enthusiastic.

"What about your trip to Ireland? Does this mean you won't be going?" she asked without emotion.

"What?" Not really noticing the question. "Ireland?" I mumbled, "I don't know....It doesn't really matter.....Isn't this great!" still full of excitement. I continued ignoring her absence of enthusiasm and went into the next room to find my tape recording of the chosen songs. A state of euphoria was taking over. I entered college on a cloud. Trying to calm myself, I found Stuart and told him the news. He gave the enthusiastic response I was hoping for. He could see how important it was for me and immediately began to joke about pop star images and the vast riches ahead. I tried very hard to concentrate on my college work but eventually gave up and decided to make that call to London. Within minutes the call was over, and I had a recording session arranged for the following week. What a thrill this was to be. I didn't really need to practice. I knew the songs backwards. I just had to bide my time a little longer until the big day arrived. My main concern was not arriving stale on the day. Over-rehearsing and losing a natural vibrancy was a definite risk. I knew all about that.

The following week arrived and I was ready for the adventure. I was trying not to build up my hopes, just to enjoy the day. If I made a fool of myself then so be it. I made my own way to Brian Reid's office and then was driven on to the Studio. The recording studio turned out to be a small room situated within Soho. It was probably very unimpressive to a professional, but it had microphones, pianos and endless wires, so to me this was musical heaven. Brian Reid had hired three session musicians to provide additional backing. Everything was set and we were ready to go. To my surprise, everything went reasonably well. It was all over within two hours. Considering I was a novice there were few problems. Everything in one take. Although one of the songs, my favorite, did not, in my opinion, have the right rhythm, there was pressure to complete the session as soon as possible. Brian was pleased that the main song was good and was now anxious to leave and save money on the session.

The recorded songs would be forwarded to Colin Blunstone. All we could do now was wait and see. I returned to Birmingham with a copy of the tapes and played them to Jenna as soon as I arrived. She seemed in a good mood, so I anxiously watched every movement in her expression. The stronger moments in the songs would, I hoped trigger some reaction. I waited. Except for the main song, the others including my favorite seemed slow. I wanted them to finish. Finally, they finished, and the room returned to silence.

"The one Colin's interested in, is good," she said politely. It wasn't a statement with conviction, and I knew they hadn't completely passed the test.

"What about the others?"

"They're nice," she said again with the same polite tone. I was angry with myself, frustrated that I had not pressed for more time, some retakes with better rhythms.

"Is that all!" I said with irritation, "just nice," I repeated. Her mood changed from happy to defensive.

"What do you want me to say?" she said, a little worried. "I like them, I really do. I've always liked them. You know that." I felt more reassured, but I continued to question her further as though in some magical way it would improve the quality of those tapes. Sensing my disappointment, she came over to me to put her arms around me. It felt patronising and I stiffened. She persisted until I relaxed. We stood there a while without talking. I touched her soft hair. Jenna responded with a ticklish nudge in my waist.

"I must go into town today," said Jenna realising the time, "I need to buy a coat."

"I'll come with you if you like," I said spontaneously.

"Will you?" she said with surprise, "you don't have to." She didn't look exactly enthused, no doubt because I would interrogate her again about the songs.

"No, I'll come..... I'll buy you lunch," I said insistently. "Can you lend me five pounds?"

"Typical," she said mockingly, "how are you going to support me in the years to come?"

"Council houses are not that expensive, are they?" I replied.

"It's you that needs counselling," she retorted. With that I moved slowly towards her with a playful but leering grin. I tried to contort my facial expression further in order to look completely deranged. Jenna looked concerned.

"Don't do that Nicholas," she pleaded, "I don't like it!" She jumped onto the bed to get out of reach. I continued to approach, raising my arms in the air like a zombie.
"Please Nick, don't....Please," she pleaded again. "You know it frightens me when you do that."

"It's no good pleading," I growled, "I'm a body snatcher and I want your body."

"You're just evil." I grabbed her ankle. She squealed. I leaned over her and then suddenly returning to normal, said "Give us a kiss."

"What a let-down," she said disappointedly, "I thought I

was going to be ravaged"

"But you are!" I growled again.

We went to look for her coat. After careful deliberation she finally decided and bought a blue, loosely tied, three quarter length outfit. It wasn't my first choice, but Jenna was clearly delighted with it, so what did I know. The next week was a week of waiting. Waiting for the telephone to ring, waiting for the post to arrive, waiting to hear something, anything from London. In the meantime, Jenna enrolled for pottery classes at the local school. The pottery classes would keep her occupied whilst I was busy in Ireland. I left for Ireland still without knowing.

I was joined on my journey by Dr. Butterworth. I think she wanted an excuse for a field trip, and this served her purpose. The goal of this trip was simple; to sample an exposed area of rocks outcropping along the cliffs of Ballycastle, a small coastal resort in Northern Ireland. We were both apprehensive about the troubles in Northern Ireland but as it turned out we experienced no real evidence of the problems. The coastal scenery was beautiful, an area that included the famous Giant's Causeway. This latter feature turned out to be less impressive than we had envisaged. Perhaps because, as geologists, we had actually seen several better examples along the Scottish west coast. Nevertheless, the trip was very enjoyable, and I was able to successfully complete my sample program.

We had travelled in Dr. Butterworth's car, a relatively old but serviceable Volkswagen. Our return trip had taken us via the ferry from Belfast, arriving in Holyhead at 5.00am, very early in the morning. As a result, Mavis sped effortlessly through the empty welsh roads and it wasn't long before I was standing outside the flat. It was only then I realised I didn't have a key and Jenna certainly wouldn't be expecting me at this time in the morning. Not wishing to disturb the neighbours with a noisy session of hammering on the door, I decided to climb on top of the flat bay window which lay like a platform below our bedroom window. The close proximity of the drainpipe made it quite accessible. What would Jenna think of being so rudely awoken at this time, especially by somebody knocking on the outside of her bedroom window? It could be anybody. Maybe I should just walk around for a couple of hours and then come back. I thought about this for a few moments, but a cold drafty wind blew through my coat, which quickly made up my mind. In any case I was looking forward to seeing her after being away a week. I balanced myself precariously on the wall but couldn't quite step onto the bay window roof as easily as I had hoped. Just then I was aware of an old man staring up at me from the pavement. He was shabbily dressed in old clothes.

"Could you give us a cup of tea when you get in," he shouted optimistically.

"Shh," I uttered, trying to appear calm and sane; as if I could, hanging from the drainpipe at 6am in the morning. At this moment I could neither get up nor down. The old man continued to stare.
"I haven't had a cup of tea for ages," he said grumpily.

I just stared at him.

"Oh buggar you!" He went on his way.

I stretched out my leg and finally got a foothold on the little roof. "I must be mad." I thought to myself and then knocked on the window. To my surprise Jenna was at the window in seconds. I beckoned her to open the window and let me in. She shook her head and gesticulated I should go back down. She would open the door. I suggested otherwise but she was insistent. I shrugged my shoulders and began the decent. It took a while. I waited at the front door until eventually I heard the latch turn.

"Come in, I'll make you a coffee," she said immediately, in a surprisingly perky voice.

"I'm sorry I forgot it would be an early ferry," I said.

"That's alright... Do you want some breakfast?" she said almost breathlessly. She did seem unusually flustered.

"Have you been running? And what took you so long? Why wouldn't you open the window for me? It would have been a lot easier for me to come in through the window." I stopped there and decided not to push my luck.

"I've got a surprise for you," I said reaching into my bag. I took out a small packet and handed it to her. "Just to prove I was thinking of you," she stared at it for a moment.

"Go on then. Open it," I said eagerly. She looked apprehensive at the tiny present and then carefully unwrapped it to reveal a small box. Inside she found a small silver chain and locket. Jenna smiled with genuine appreciation.

"It's lovely," she said holding it against her chest. "It's really lovely." She put it down on the bed continuing to stare at the locket but almost reluctant to touch it."

"It won't bite....You like it then?" I asked wishing to confirm all was well.

"Yes, I really do." She looked at me with her large brown eyes.

"Do I get my breakfast now?" I enquired jokingly.

"For this you get a champagne breakfast, if you want." She laughed. "But first, I have a surprise for you." She walked towards the mantelpiece and picked up a letter and passed it to me. It was from London. Jenna went through into the kitchen. "Is it good news!" she shouted. The same thought was in my mind too. "Was it good or bad news?" I immediately saw Brian Reid's name at the bottom. This confirmed it was the letter I'd been waiting for. I scanned the single page just looking for the key words. I took a deep breath.

"It is good news!!" I shouted back in astonishment. "It says Colin Blunstone would like to record "If you really don't know". A recording date has been set and the music is being scored for the backing arrangements."

"That's wonderful news," said Jenna with a congratulatory tone.

"It is isn't it," I said still staring at the letters in disbelief. "I'll ring him to see if I can be there for the recording session. Surely they wouldn't mind."

Jenna returned into the room with a strange shaped vase. "Want to see what I've made at pottery class?" It was a very unusual shape. I tried to think of a very tactful answer. In no way did I wish to spoil the mood of this moment.

***

During the next two weeks I heard nothing more from

London. I was getting a little anxious. Jenna and I kept busy, however, both meeting friends and with college work. Stuart and Beth invited us to a concert with Oscar Peterson at the Birmingham town hall. I also went to Sheffield to rehearse with the newly formed band, all of which provided a welcome distraction. The absence of news from London, however, was ominous and I was beginning to suspect the worst. It was Thursday evening and I was staying up late waiting for Jenna to come back from the pottery lesson. I sat on the edge of the bed, hunched over my guitar. I made a decision to ring Brian Reid first thing in the morning. Jenna finally returned. I heard her making coffee in the kitchen before finally appearing in the living room.

"Successful evening?" I asked, and without waiting for a reply began to play a few chords.

"Yes, I did actually we've…" She stopped and then in an irritated voice asked, "Can you stop that for a moment when I'm talking to you. It's very impolite."

I stopped. She continued. "I just wanted to tell you that we've been invited to a party at Victor's house." She announced the news almost formally. Victor was one my research colleagues in the department.
"Really?" I said a little puzzled, "how did you get to know about this?" It seemed unusual since he hardly knew Jenna.

"Stuart told me," she said, almost proudly," he passed on the message to me at College yesterday… I forgot to tell you."

"First I've heard about it," I said, slightly miffed at being left out. "I wonder why he never mentioned it himself?"

Jenna was still irritated and began noisily collecting her

books off the table. "You're always playing that damned guitar. I'm surprised anything gets into your brain sometimes," she said angrily. "All you think about is music and little green space invaders. You never think about me." It was clear where this conversation was heading. I wasn't in the mood and decided to go next door to watch television.

"Don't you leave me here, without saying anything," she said demandingly. I remained silent and sat deliberately concentrating on the television. "Are you going to talk to me or am I just to be ignored," she said again with increased frustration.

"You don't have to talk to me like that," I said, irritated.

"Well why don't you say something to me?" she demanded.

"I can't really, there's nothing I can say that you actually want to hear," I said defensively, "shall we talk about the weekend shopping. Is that what you want to hear?"

"Typical!" she shouted with exasperation, "You don't even contribute to that properly. It's me that has to sort it out. You get looked after very well by me," said forcefully. Her voice was becoming increasingly patronising and matronly. I had no defense for these remarks so all I could do was to wait for them to stop. I continued to stare at the television and said nothing.

"Why don't you speak to me!!" she screamed. I was beginning to worry if it would ever subside, but nothing short of a marriage proposal would stop this, and that would be stupid. She moved towards the cutlery drawer in the kitchen and clumsily yanked it open. Out sprang the drawer and all its contents onto the floor with a loud clatter. She didn't look surprised. No doubt she thought the noise was appropriate for the occasion.

"Now look," she said accusingly, "now come and pick this up. You made me do this." I didn't move. She was angry, very angry. As she marched passed me, close by the chair I instinctively moved forward out of reach, expecting her to strike out at any moment. She gave me a disdainful look and then went into the bedroom. Nothing else was said for the rest of the evening.

She never came back into the kitchen, so I remained there watching television. I stayed there because I also felt angry. I felt angry but I didn't know why. The tone of Jenna's voice certainly didn't give me any incentive to go in there and apologise. And apologise for what? All I was guilty of was trying to be honest. I didn't want to lead her on, say something I couldn't follow through with. I couldn't just say, "Yes dear, of course dear, you're quite right dear, no problem, let's get married dear." On the other hand there was a problem. This stubborn detachment of mine, was driving her nuts. I had to change. I took it all too seriously. So what, if I change my mind tomorrow. There was surely no harm in telling her how beautiful she was; how I ached to see her move; the shape of her eyes; the neat well defined line of her mouth. "Tell her tonight. Tell her tonight you love her, because tonight you do. Who cares about tomorrow."

The television blared out at me. Whilst I had been dreaming, there had been a change in program and I hadn't realised. I saw the light beneath the bedroom door switch off. On the television the music of MASH suddenly intruded, and I was distracted. I watched the introduction and was hooked. Half an hour later, after a last cup of coffee, I tiptoed into the bedroom. Jenna was fast asleep. I undressed quietly and slid gently into bed. She didn't wake.

When I awoke it was 8.30am and Jenna was dressed and virtually ready to go to college.

"I just wish for once you'd think about me!" she scowled. I rubbed my eyes in an attempt to revive myself.

"Are we late?" I asked. "Why didn't you wake me?" I tried to reach for her arm but I was too late. She had her coat on and was ready to leave.

"Don't forget about this evening," she said coldly. "If you want to go to Victor's party, I'll see you back here at seven o'clock; otherwise I'll assume you have made other arrangements. I'll catch the bus." The message was strong, she was clearly upset. I heard the door slam and she was gone. I got up with a sore head.

It was fortunate research projects did not usually demand a punctual arrival each morning. During the day I thought a lot about our relationship, and although I didn't understand all the reasons for Jenna's apparent anguish, I had definitely decided to open up to her. After all she didn't really know how I truly felt. In fact, I was quite looking forward to this evening. This would be a turning point, "Of course it would," I said to myself, "But one thing at a time". I'd forgotten to ring Brian Reid. I needed to know what was going on and it was time to find out. I found a pay phone outside the department and made the call. It was a brave thing to do considering the possible outcome and by the time he answered I was feeling quite anxious. His tone was quite sombre as he explained at length that Colin had written a song of his own and now wished to record this instead. At this stage there was nothing more could be done. I was mortified. It was terribly disappointing. I walked dejectedly back to the department and slumped into my chair.

There are some moments that only a piano will help you feel better. It was five o'clock and there was just time for ten minutes on the ol'faithful upright. It usually helped. So, I began. The notes just flowed like velvet. It seemed especially good this evening. A chord of D minor flowed effortlessly into B flat and unusual inclusions of E flat were starting to suggest themselves, energising the mood. The notes developed, and the rhythm increased. It was intense and important. I continued like this trying to blot out the news of the telephone call.

"Wow this feels good," I said out loud feeling relieved. The sound of my own voice suddenly made me check the time. I'd been playing nearly two hours. "It's a quarter to seven!" I gasped. "Oh no!" I moaned. I shut the piano lid and ran. This was hopelessly late. I leapt into the car and started the engine. I pushed down heavily on the accelerator pedal. The car unwillingly responded. It was ten years old. It wasn't used to being hurried along in such haste. I reached the flat only 15 minutes late, but she was gone. A note was waiting for me on the kitchen table. It simply read.

"I waited until seven o'clock."

I changed as quickly as I could. The party was only a few streets away, but I took the car to try and make up more time. Then I remembered I had to take a bottle of wine as an entrance fee. After a small detour I finally arrived outside Victor's house, one and a half hours late. "She's going to murder me," I suddenly thought. The front door was open so I let myself in. The noise was deafening, the music was far too loud. Two or three couples filled the hallway obviously trying to escape. I saw Victor and made my way over to talk to him.

"Thanks for the invitation!" I shouted, passing over the

bottle of wine. "Sorry I'm late." I could barely make myself heard.

"That's alright," said Victor jovially, his body moving in a sort of involuntary manner to the beat of the music.

"Have you seen Jenna?" I shouted, putting my hands to my mouth, in an attempt to make myself heard.

"She's around here somewhere.... With Stuart I think?" He gave back the bottle of wine and said, "Could you put this in the kitchen for me and then just help yourself."

"Ok thanks, I will," I left him dancing.

The room was dark and I was having difficulty recognising people. As I stepped into the kitchen area it was even darker. In the gloom I could make out several people, but only two caught my eye. The sight of them froze me to the spot. In the corner, huddled close together Stuart and Jenna were engaged in a passionate embrace, his hands fondly caressing her body. His hands were everywhere, their mouths fervently pressed together. I continued to watch them for a few seconds, transfixed, rooted, I couldn't move a muscle. I began to tremble, and a tremendous buzzing noise filled my head. The noise seemed to grow uncontrollably. It seemed my head was going to burst. This couldn't be real. As I watched for those few brief agonising seconds I felt hurt beyond any boundaries I had believed possible. It was like someone had opened up an artery, my life-blood flowing out, spilling out all that had been so dear to me...... And now there seemed no way of stopping it. I turned my head away and, somehow, I managed to walk back into the living room. My mind began a tormented sequence of thoughts.

"Nothing yet was properly established. Perhaps it was just

one drunken cuddle, a single stolen kiss," I said unconvincingly to myself. I was going to leave but I had to look again. I walked once more towards the doorway, now shivering almost uncontrollably. They were still locked in each other's arms. The pain was indescribable. A surge of anger began to rise inside me. I thought about going to face them, but the rage was starting to take over. I felt capable of anything. Even murder. I turned away for the second time and slowly moved back towards the front door.

Once outside I didn't want to leave. I stood motionless for a while staring blankly into the darkness. What else could I do. I felt empty, lost. Out here there seemed no direction. I moved further towards the front of the garden and then looked back at the house. A familiar figure stood by the front door. It was Beth. I had somehow assumed she wouldn't have been here. We looked at each other and I waited for her to say something. Something soothing. Something to explain this horror. In the poor light I couldn't be sure what she was thinking or feeling. She said nothing. I was about to step towards her, ask her what it was all about. She must know. I hesitated and for some unexplained reason, stepped back and then pointed to the window of the kitchen.
"They're in there, you know. They're…" I said in a faltering voice. I couldn't finish the words. Beth didn't react. She was impassive like a statue. It was like a dream. It didn't feel real. I turned towards the car. Suddenly I heard Beth's voice shout out to me. I stopped.

"What do your little aliens tell you now, Nick?.....What have they got say about this?........I'm waiting, ….tell me....." I didn't turn round.

I remember very little of the journey back, except deciding I couldn't stay in the flat that night. My mind racing, I couldn't concentrate on anything. At the flat I paced the floor incessantly. I just couldn't calm myself. I stared around at all the familiar things of Jenna's. They all seemed so precious. How could I leave them? I managed, at last, to scramble a few of my things together and threw them in the car. I had decided to drive through the night to Sheffield and to stay with Brian. Brian and I had become friends and what I needed now was a friendly voice.

As I closed the door and made ready to go, the passenger door opened. It was Jenna. She must have walked back from the party. Somebody must have told her. She got in the car and sat next to me.

"Where are you going?" she demanded.

"I am going to Sheffield," I said without emotion. "You know why."

"No, I don't." she replied.

"Oh, don't you!" I said in astonishment. "Is that so.....Well, I've known about you and Stuart for a long time and I've had enough. Now it's time for me to go." Of course, I knew nothing at all about this, but somehow I had to try and find out more. I was willing to try anything.

"You mean it's over between us?" she said in horror.

"Yes!" I replied emphatically. The word seemed so final. I hadn't thought any of this through and I wasn't really sure what I wanted to do. I was still shocked. I just wanted to find out more.

"Nick don't go, I love you." She seemed to find a tearful voice rather too quickly. It sounded rehearsed. I didn't believe it.

"I've had enough and I want to go," I said angrily. I was trying to find more hurtful words. Something to really make her ache with pain.

"You can't go now. Not after all this time we have been together." Her demanding tone was beginning to reappear.

"Well, I am. Could you leave now? I'll pick up the rest of my things when I get back." She was not moved by this.

"Look, come in and have a cup of coffee." She leaned over to kiss me, but all I wanted to do was hurt.

"Get off!" I said roughly, and pushed her away. Suddenly the expression on Jenna's face changed.

"You know Stuart loves me." she said proudly, "He's going to leave his wife and marry me." Another bombshell. This hit me hard. How long had this been going on?

"So that's why you were so keen on me going to Ireland." I said, starting to piece things together.

"I didn't want you to go, if you remember." No, I didn't remember, but she was confirming my worst suspicions.

"I knew what would happen." she continued. "He's been so attentive and gentle with me. It was like meeting you again for the first time." she said candidly. I was surprised she was telling me all this, and so matter of fact. The throbbing in my head was deafening. I could barely hear myself think.

"How many times have you slept with him?" I stupidly asked, hardly daring to listen to the answer. Jenna shuffled and looked uncomfortable.

"Oh, I can't remember." she said irritably. "Since the first time we went to their house. He met me upstairs as I went to the loo. He kissed me then." Suddenly I just couldn't listen to anymore. She stopped.

"Get out!" I choked, "Get out now!!" I repeated tearfully. She didn't seem to realise how much I cared. How much I needed her. How much I treasured every moment with her. How much her words were now unmercifully cutting me to pieces.

She got out of the car. "You bastard," she shouted slamming the door. "Go on then, run home to mummy!"

I clenched the steering wheel and rammed the gear stick into first and with an undignified lurch sped away into the night. The roads were clear, but my eyes were filled with tears. I drove on remorselessly. I needed to get away, to go home. She seemed proud of what she'd done. The tone of her voice had no regret., as though she didn't care. Just annoyed that I wouldn't stay. I stared at the road ahead, feeling every mile I was putting between us. At the same time, it began to dawn on me just how many opportunities she must have had to be unfaithful. All the times I was away on field trips, her regular pottery classes, and all starting a year ago. Stuart and Beth had seemed so happy together. I never dreamed there was a problem. Or was he just being greedy. His appetite for the ladies was unquestionable. The images came flooding through. Victor's gloomy kitchen played over and over. Nothing would block it out.

"Go away!" I suddenly yelled out loud and gripped the steering wheel even harder. "Go away," I mumbled again. Self-pity was beginning to take over.

It was well after midnight when I arrived in the Sheffield

area, too late to intrude on Brian, so I would have to make my way home for the night. Since my father's retirement, my parents had moved house and were now living in a community of flats on the opposite side of Rotherham. They were still up, and greeted me with surprise. I'd told them the story.

Curiously, the next day I felt better, the new surroundings seeming to strike an optimistic note. The high drama of the previous night had subsided considerably. I was relieved. Surrounded by family I was somehow managing to keep a clearer head. My mother immediately dismissed Jenna and spoke of her only in derogatory tones.

"You just want to forget her," she said with ease. "It's too early for you to settle down. You ought to play the field a bit more." It seemed strange to hear my mother use the term 'playing the field', especially since prior to that everything connected with girlfriends had been closely scrutinised with high moral tones.

"There's a nice young girl moved in at number 7, two flats across from us. I get on with her ever so well." she suggested breezily. "Why don't you take her out?"
"She's alright, isn't she Eric," looking over to my father.

"She's alright," he replied with indifference.

"I'll ask her what she's doing, when I next see her." I was amazed that my mother should feel it necessary to do this. It made me feel uncomfortable.

"No, that's alright mum," I said, trying not to offend. "Talk about out of the frying pan."

"Well, she seems a nice girl to me. She always comes and chats," said mum again.

I was, now, curious. Tonight, however, I only had plans to meet up with Brian. An evening almost guaranteed to be good straightforward fun and an opportunity to talk music. And it was. We met at a small pub in the centre of Sheffield together with a few of his friends. They were steelworkers, landscape gardeners, car mechanics, quite different to myself, but they were friendly and I enjoyed the stories they told. It was only during the journey home, whilst alone, did it become difficult. I could only think of one thing. Jenna had telephoned my mother during the day. She didn't tell me, but I overheard the conversation and so I had interrupted and insisted on talking with her. Unlike the night before, her voice was weak and quavering. She was sobbing. I was still angry, but yet I wanted to make her feel better. Clearly, she wanted me back and in my heart I wanted to go back. The sound of her voice was so familiar and soothing. I gave a cautious reply, nothing definite. I had decided to stay Sunday night and make an early start Monday morning.

After a difficult journey, I finally arrived in Birmingham and went directly to the polytechnic to try and meet up with Jenna in between her early lectures. It was 10.00am already and as yet nobody had seen her. My suspicions aroused, I marched over to the Research Department to speak to Stuart, my pace beginning to quicken, as I suspected he wasn't there. Victor saw me and the anger building up inside me.

"Where are you going now?" he asked.

"To the flat," I said loudly.

Victor grabbed hold of my shoulder. "Before you go back there you have to calm down," he said in a concerned way.

"We're all sorry about what's been going on. We could see

it was only a matter of time before you found out," he continued in a sympathetic tone.

"How long have you known?" I asked curiously.

"Ever since she arrived. At first, we assumed Stuart was her boyfriend," said Victor impassively.

"How could she!" I exclaimed. I was trembling again. I'd thought after being found out they wouldn't risk being together again. I'd never considered that he might stay with her over the weekend, especially after speaking to me so sincerely on the telephone. The limits to her betrayal seemed boundless. I stared at a geological hammer laying on the desk in front of me. I picked it up.

"Put it down Nick," said Victor quietly but firmly. I ignored him and went out to the car.

My mood was black. I was filled with hate and I wanted revenge. As I approached the flat, I checked the cars parked along the street, looking for signs of Stuart's blue De Cheveux. It was there, not parked outside the flat but at the top of the road, out of obvious view. The site of his car practically destroyed me. It seemed the whole situation was totally out of my control. Stuart and Jenna seemed able to twist the knife at will. I made my way towards the flat as though stalking my prey, careful not to make a sound. The front door key turned silently, and I was inside at the foot of the stairs. I still gripped the hammer in my hand. I climbed three of the lower stairs and as I did, I heard mumbled voices. I climbed another two and was now at the floor level of the landing and would be able to see into the kitchen area. Slowly I raised my head. It felt awkward, like I was a spy. I chastised myself for allowing myself to feel this way in my own flat.

"He's going to pay for this!" my anger turning towards Stuart.

Now in full view I could see Stuart and Jenna locked in a frenzy of love making. They were both pressed against the kitchen wall but only partly dressed. Stuart was panting, almost out of breath hurriedly trying to remove the rest of her clothing. Jenna had only her maroon jumper on, my favorite jumper. She lifted it up for him, exposing her breasts. He paused momentarily to stare at them. Jenna grabbed him by the neck and pulled him onto her, almost smothering him as he wrestled to get his breath.

Just as before, I stood in disbelief. My eyes watered with the horror of what I saw. It was a nightmare. I sank back against the wall of the stairway. I swallowed hard two or three times trying to compose myself. But I was allowed no respite. The sound of Jenna's quiet groans were quite audible. Groans of pleasure which desecrated any feelings I may have had for her. The anguish and hurt was almost unbearable and a feeling of nausea and sickness hit my stomach. I felt I was going to vomit so turned to step out into the street. The fresh air pulled me round and after a deep breath it went away. I still had the hammer clenched tight in my fist. Now I was ready. I turned and ran back up the stairs. As I reached the top, Jenna shouted out.

"Who's that!" I didn't respond but just began aimlessly shouting obscenities, loud and angry, "Bastards", "Whore." I was like a wounded animal squealing helplessly.

"Where's Stuart!" I demanded. Jenna was trying to dress. "Where is he?" I demanded again. My words were cold.

I started the search. He was no longer in the kitchen. Jenna tried to grab me, but I raised my arm in defense, revealing the hammer. She cried out in panic "Nick don't......Don't do it!!" My eyes must have been bulging, crazed. I was mad now, out of control. I was going to hurt him. I rushed into the bedroom. The window was open. I heard the sound of someone landing on the ground outside. I reached the window to see him running like a scared rabbit. I smiled a perverted grimaced smile well satisfied that he was scared. Bravely Jenna came over and took the hammer away. She spoke softly to me.

"I didn't think you'd be coming back."

"Is that why he tried to hide his car," I rallied, but it sounded like the beginning of a childish squabble. After everything else that had happened such a conversation sounded trivial. She didn't answer. She searched for something else to say but couldn't. I looked up at the ceiling in defiance, trying not to look at her, desperately holding back the hurt.

"I saw you, through the banisters," I said, and as I said these words the pain come flooding back and tears began to flow down my cheeks. "I was standing on the stairs and I saw you," I said again. "Was it good, was he gentle enough?" Saying these things was hurting me more than her. I broke down and the tears began to flow uncontrollably. She took hold of me and held me close to her.

"I want you Nicholas, I only want you."

I buried my head in her shoulder and neck and could smell her natural perfume. It felt so comforting and I wanted her again. She was so much into my system, so much a part of me I couldn't pull away. For this brief moment I wanted to enjoy the warmth, nothing else mattered. She stroked my head like a child.

"I never knew you felt like this about me. I never knew if you wanted me or not," she spoke quietly. I remained there, in a kneeling position on the floor trying to think what I should do next. Strangely the thoughts of reconciliation did not last long. I just couldn't quell the anguish. I couldn't stay. In fact, I wouldn't stay now even if she begged. I stood up, briefly looked at her anxious expression and then turned to leave. As I walked slowly down the stairs Jenna shouted out from the landing.

"But you never said anything!"

"You never told me you loved me."

I stepped outside once more into the fresh air, took a deep breath and walked away.

CHAPTER SIX

It was now time to change direction. If I believed there were doubts before, then there were certainly plenty of doubts to think about now. It was laughable to consider any other course of action than a change in direction. I made plans to move out of the flat and back to the room I'd previously had with Brian and Judy. They didn't seem to mind at all and were intrigued by the events that had befallen me. It was only then that I noticed communications with Jenna and Stuart had but for a few absolute essentials ceased and it appeared to be me who was most visibly suffering. Stuart, unfortunately occupied the desk opposite to mine so I couldn't avoid him. His appearance took on a sinister air. Complete with beard and wrinkled seafaring skin tones he fitted the image of a pirate very easily. He would give me a sneering smile now and then if our eyes should happen to meet.

"Happy now with what you've done?" I sneered.
"You are so naïve, Nick," responded Stuart "Every time you took a trip to Ireland, Sheffield, wherever, me and others from her department paid her a visit. Even today, there is probably someone at your flat. I've screwed her a hundred times over this last year….She's insatiable!" His voice was flat and lacked any remorse.

I got up from my seat and marched away. The words throbbed in my brain.

"Was this really true," I pondered. "Oh my God! If it's true!"

I went immediately to the flat. There was no one there. I

grabbed everything that was left of my things and went back to Brain and Judy's house.

Despite all that had happened I found that I missed her. I missed her so very much. At first it was just an uncomfortable feeling which I thought I could easily avoid by simply thinking of more pleasant things. Like a bad dream, one night's good sleep and then we start over again. I genuinely thought it would be that easy. But I was wrong. As the obvious painful thoughts returned, I found myself restless, unable to sit, senselessly shifting from chair to chair, room to room. Uncontrollably the pain just grew. I was unnerved by the intensity. It became that there were no particular thoughts attached to this feeling, no centre or physical attribute I could focus on, just pain. I knew now what it was like to be clinically depressed. For all I could tell it would last forever.

Walking helped a little, so I walked. The walking was quick and urgent, anything to deflect the upwelling of discomfort in my head. I walked all the streets in the neighbourhood many times, all day and all night, fearing to stop, unless I was sure I was absolutely exhausted and could hopefully fall asleep. I barely noticed I had lost weight and developed pains in my knees. It didn't seem to matter. As the days passed nothing seemed to matter. Only this tremendous feeling of loss and anxiety that had taken over.

On one level it was quite amusing I should be in this situation. But on another level, it actually made me angry to endure this. This made me more determined that I was not going to let this thing beat me. One way or another I was going to crawl out of this, and as fast as possible. The trouble was I felt like death and without an appetite.

Yes, it was clear things had changed, and as a part of that change had to be finding new friends. By a curious coincidence I discovered that Brian and Philippa, two friends from schooldays, had moved into the tall block of flats immediately opposite my parents. This made it easy to visit them when I went home at weekends. Consequently, it was inevitable that I would visit home more often and, similarly, that I should eventually meet up with the girl next door. In fact, at this stage I had only seen her at a distance as she went to and fro from the flats. The flats were arranged in a row and the entrance driveway to the flats passed close by my parent's window enabling us to observe all who came and went. In this way I watched her several times pass by.

On one occasion I watched her from the kitchen window as she parked her red Volvo saloon car. She had blonde, medium length hair curving under in a neat and attractive style. She was dressed in a business-like fashion with a straight grey skirt and jacket. Despite her formal dress she clearly had an attractive face with beautiful wide set eyes. Although I wanted to deny it, I was curious. It could only help. But how was I going to meet her.

"Something interesting out there?" came a voice suddenly. It was my mother and she had caught me red handed in full snooping pose. I felt silly. I stepped back a little too quickly and put my hand down on something soft and sticky. "Mind that toast!" she said. But it was too late. Without saying anything I went to the bathroom to clean up and plan my next move. Returning to the lounge I sat down on the settee next to my father smoking his twentieth cigarette of the day. The smoke was very conspicuous, so I moved further away to a chair on the other side of the room. I sat hugging a big orange cushion desperately plotting but nothing came to mind. It was nearly lunch time, so I got up again to help my mother with the sandwiches.

"I'm going to meet your friend next door," I announced boldly.

"Oh yes," she said suspiciously, "You mean Natasha?"

"So that's her name." I said with interest. "That helps."

"When are you meeting her?"

"I don't know yet," I said, "I'm working on it."

"Why not knock on her door and ask to borrow something."

"Hmm, not a bad idea mum," and with that immediately made my way to the front door.

"I thought you were helping me with the lunch?" she said disappointedly.

"Nope, I've got a date," I said with misplaced confidence. As I walked the short distance to her front door, I felt conspicuous as though everyone in the block of flats opposite was watching me. I rang the bell and waited. Through the glass door I could see a figure approach. To my surprise a very different, but none the less, pretty young lady opened the door. She had long dark hair and a refined appearance. She smiled

"Yes?" she enquired politely.

"Erm. Is Natasha there please? I asked awkwardly.

"Yes, step in for a minute." I walked into the hallway.

"Natasha it's for you!" she said sharply and then disappeared into the living room. Natasha came out of another room.

"Hello," she said warmly. I began my story.

"I'm in need of a London A to Z. I don't suppose you have one. My mother suggested you might be able to help out," I said embarrassingly. She listened politely. I felt sure she could see right through this subterfuge.

"I'll see what I can do," clearly amused she disappeared into her room and returned with the book. The moment was disappearing fast and I wasn't making much progress. I took hold of the book and thanked her, promising to return it shortly. It was over. The door closed and I stood outside. I looked up at the high-rise flats on the opposite side of the carpark. I felt sure Brian and Philippa were looking down on me.

That evening I made arrangements to meet Brian and Philippa at a local pub. We chatted endlessly. There was so much to catch up on, especially the news that they were finally going to get married. Philippa was slim and had very long, beautiful dark hair which always fell seductively over her shoulders. She also had a vibrant personality and, most conspicuously, a wicked sense of humour which she used to tease us all mercilessly. Brian was tall and slim but more placid and very able to take things in his stride. They knew quite a lot about Jenna and seemed genuinely sympathetic.

"Do you hate her?" asked Philippa concerned.

"Yes, I suppose so," I replied hesitantly. I still wasn't sure.

"What about the girl next door you mentioned," said Brian trying to inject a little more optimism.

"Yeah... not bad,"

An attractive group of girls entered the pub and paraded passed us.

"What about one of them?" asked Philippa in a provocative manner. We all watched them as they began to settle down close by.

"Not for me. Not tonight."

"Pity," said Brian sensing a lost opportunity.

"It's too late for you Brian," said Philippa, staking her claim.

"But not for Nick," said purposefully pointing to one of them at the bar. "It's your round isn't it" Signalling the opportunity. Reluctantly I agreed. It did look like there was a small chance of something.

"But I'm not going to chat anybody up," I insisted. Once at the bar I was served very quickly. They watched me as I fumbled with my wallet. I returned.

"Did she say anything?" they both asked as I sat.

"Didn't get a chance," I admitted. A moment later I felt a tap on my shoulder. It was the girl who was stood at the bar.

"Is this yours?" she said indignantly, and then thrust my passport photograph onto the table. "Please don't leave your calling card for me, you nasty little boy!" she scowled and then immediately marched off.

"It must have......." I spluttered trying to say something. "I didn't......."

After the initial stunned silence Philippa started to laugh. I was left high and dry and totally embarrassed. I looked back over at Philippa. "I'm beginning to go off females." "Liar," retorted Philippa.

The evening passed and we said our farewells. I slowly made my way across the carpark when I was suddenly dazzled by some car headlights coming straight at me. I leapt out of the way to notice it was Natasha's red Volvo. She parked in her usual spot and stepped out of the car.

"Hello again," she said chirpily, "sorry about that. I'll get you next time maybe?"

I smiled, trying not to look flustered.

"Did you get what you wanted from that book?"

"Yes, I did thanks very much. I'll get it now for you," I said pointing to my parents flat. "Won't be a moment." I grabbed the book from the hallway where it was still lying unopened and walked back to Natasha's flat. The door was open, and the light was on. I knocked lightly on the door. Natasha quickly reappeared with a towel under her arm.

"Do you swim?" she asked very directly.

"Yes," I said cautiously.

"Would you like to go swimming now?"

"Are you serious? Its 10.30pm," I exclaimed.

"Yes I know. I just feel like going. Do you want to come?" She said with a big smile.

"Where?" I said a little perplexed.

"The Aquarious is open......It's a night club as well." I accepted the invitation and rushed off to get my things. My mother watched on curiously trying to take a modern perspective but still maintaining an element of suspicion. I tried to keep out of my father's view. Just before I left my mother whispered, "Jenna telephoned." My heart missed a beat. It was strange how her name seemed to affect me, eager and yet angry at the same time. I attempted an indifferent tone as I responded.

"Oh?" hoping she would provide more news.

"She was crying. Sobbing, in fact, and said that she wasn't feeling very well."

"What did you say?" trying to imply annoyance.

"I was short with her, of course, but said I would pass on the message. After what she did to you, I wouldn't give her the time of day, if I could help it. I found it hard to be nice to her. Never really liked her."

My mother's comments were to be expected, but yet, secretly I was thrilled that she had called. Just to hear her name. Yet one telephone call wasn't going to ease the pain.

"Is that all she said?" I asked.

"Yes, but don't worry about that. Go on and enjoy yourself."

Despite this unexpected reminder, Natasha and I really did enjoy ourselves. We got on surprisingly well, sharing the same silly humour. She was very attractive with a slim waist and curves that I never knew existed before but delighted to know now. Her milky smooth skin texture was also very attractive, quite different in some ways to

Jenna. After the swimming was over, we stayed on to listen to the Cabaret. It was my first experience of a night club and live entertainment of this kind. We sat at a table and listened to Dave Berry sing the Crying Game. His performance was most impressive, almost exactly the same as I had seen it before on Top of the Pops. We talked about almost everything and I got to know a lot about Natasha's background. She told me her parents lived in Nottingham, although originally had moved over from Warrington some years ago. She had done well at grammar school and achieved good grades in her exams. However, it had not been the same success at College where she had left before completing her course. Apparently, a long standing, relationship with a boyfriend had broken up at a delicate time during examinations and had consequently lost heart. Feeling in a similar situation myself, now, I felt some sympathy with her. It didn't seem as if she had a boyfriend at present. She presently had a job selling houses and drove out to various sites to spend her day in the show house where she would answer enquiries and show people around. Apparently, it had not been easy to find any kind of job. She moved up to Rotherham to be nearer her work and to establish some independence from her parents, sharing her flat with Lisa, the young lady who had answered the door. Lisa had a degree and was now in a management training position with C&A. Natasha obviously liked Lisa and respected her abilities. Lisa was also infatuated with the love of her life and described a mysterious young man of good looks, and cool charm and a power to dictate terms. I was becoming jealous of the description of him. They were all the qualities I would like and didn't have. Natasha, I suspected, already knew something of my own circumstance from her acquaintance with my mother. There was no problem, therefore in making some reference to my current situation with Jenna. It was with relief that I could discuss the matter. She seemed willing to listen and help sort things through. She seemed more sensitive than Jenna to the everyday give and take of dealing with people. Jenna, by contrast, was always quick to confront. I could already sense Natasha felt just as much for other people's feelings as she did her own. I really felt I was discovering a new friend. It felt good. Perhaps this was the progress I was looking for.

We finally arrived back at the flats late in the morning. The car park was dark and silent and still. We tiptoed to a doorway and then embraced to say goodnight. She responded with a kiss.

"Shall I see you tomorrow?" I whispered.

"I'm working until 12.00am. I could meet you at the Golden Ball at lunch time if you like."

The arrangements were agreed, and we crept back to our respective flats. I woke up the next morning with an air of anticipation and apprehension. I was a little nervous of the forthcoming meeting with Natasha because the last evening had gone so well. In the cold light of day perhaps it would be different. The fear of rejection began to loom, but it was all unfounded as the lunch went very well. In fact, as the day progressed it was Natasha who initiated the next venue for the forthcoming weekend.

I travelled down to Birmingham with a new sense of optimism arriving late at the house. Brian called to me as I made my way upstairs.

"We had a visitor earlier. There's a letter for you." He spoke with a particular tone in his voice. As he handed it over the writing was immediately recognisable. I took it upstairs to open it. The plaintive tone of the letter was sad. Despite this, there was no reference to her affair with Stuart. She seemed to make no reference to what had happened or whether it was still happening. As far as I was concerned, since I had left, I had to assume she was continuing her relationship with Stuart, and perhaps others. This thought was always with me and I couldn't build any bridges of reconciliation until this was out in the open and clarified. Perhaps Stuart was exaggerating this wild story.

The next day I arose and dressed quickly and prepared my books for college. On opening the front door, I felt a fine drizzle in the air. It was a grey day and I wondered if the car would start. There were water droplets all over the outside of the car which would no doubt affect the battery. In this sort of dampness, the chance of a quick getaway was minimal. I wiped the outside of the car side window to suddenly reveal a face staring back at me. It was Jenna. She had managed to open the window and let herself in. She seemed sleepy and could only slowly lift her head as she tried to smile. I opened the door.

"I don't feel well Nicholas......." She put her hand to her mouth as though she was going to be sick. "I don't know what's wrong with me.......I just don't feel well." She spoke with an anxious tone. "What shall I do.....tell me what to do," she said again with concern.

At first, I didn't know for sure whether this was a small melodrama or not. I decided it wasn't.

"What are you doing here?" I asked, as I helped her out of the car.

"Help me, Nick," The tone was almost rehearsed and set me on my guard.

"Come in and have a drink of something," I said, without emotion. "How long have you been like this?"

"A few days......" she began, "I can't keep anything down, nothing at all, and I keep getting stomach pains low down here." She pointed to the side of her stomach."

"Have you been taking anything unusual?" I asked, trying to clarify things.

"Of course not!" she retorted sharply.

"Ok, I only asked." We went into the kitchen and she sat down slowly and carefully on one of the chairs. She suddenly wretched as though about to be sick. I passed her a glass of water. It was of little use. No sooner had she sipped a little of it, than her stomached heaved again. This wasn't one of her melodramas.

"Let me take you to the hospital," I suggested, now with a real sense of concern. She groaned with the pain and then slumped back in the chair. She looked pale. I helped her up and led her out to the car. Quickly wiping the electronics under the bonnet, I tried to start it. It started. Driving fearfully fast and screaming silently at the traffic I was at the hospital in minutes. She was led away, weak and still in pain, to a cubicle for observation by the doctors. I watched her disappear. I was beginning to worry, sensing how ill she was.

Eventually a doctor re-appeared. He went over to the nurse who then pointed over to me. Wasting no time, he came and told me she had a burst appendix and would have to operate immediately. The nurse asked if I knew when she last ate. I told her I didn't really know. The nurse made a note on her pad.

"You can wait with her now if you like," she said. I nodded eagerly.

I wanted to be with her. She lay alone, sedated in a cubicle away from the reception area. I took hold of her hand and we waited. After a short while a porter appeared, and she was wheeled away. She was now in their care. I took a seat in the large reception hall which acted as a waiting area. The visitors came and went, bearing flowers and all manner of sweets and fruit, shepherding children backwards and forwards. An endless stream of unknown faces. It was during this time I came to realise how dear Jenna really was to me and just how important our relationship was. I felt I was losing her again for the second time.

The echo of noises within the large hall began to fade as I started to feel drowsy. The fingers on the large clock, hung high on the wall moved slowly, stubbornly refusing to be hurried by the anxious stares. After what seemed an eternity the nurse finally appeared and gave me the news. The operation had been a success. It was a great relief and I immediately thanked her enthusiastically for all their help. I thought about staying a little longer, but it was too early to see her and was advised to come back later during normal visiting hours. It just remained for me to go home and get some sleep. I stepped out into the late evening air and took a deep breath. It had been a long day.

The next day and after a restless night I arrived back at the hospital. Carrying flowers and chocolates I walked towards the main entrance feeling satisfied in my own mind that she was going to be alright. Glancing at the row of cars parked close to the main entrance I was unnerved to see a familiar blue De Cheveux. I checked the registration. It was Stuart's. I quickened my pace and marched into the reception. Following the endless signs and corridors I made my way as soon as possible to the ward, ready to confront Stuart at any turn. I reached the ward without sighting him. I stared down the line of beds, trying to control an increasing feeling of anger. It took two or three attempts before I could actually locate Jenna midway along the left side. "She must have called him," I said to myself. "How else could he have known? What other explanation could there have been?" I walked up to the bedside determined to ask some pointed questions. Instead I was stopped, physically shocked to see how poorly she looked; so pale and weak. She was asleep, but then opened her eyes and feebly spoke a few words.

"Glad you could come," she whispered.

"I've come to take you to the dance." She tried to smile.

"Not tonight."

I noticed there were some tubes coming out of the bed that were presumably attached to her in some way, but I didn't ask. Temporarily all problems were forgotten as I stared helplessly at her pale and fragile condition.

"How are you?" her voice barely audible.

"Oh, I'm ok, don't you worry about me. I'm only jealous of you lying around in bed doing nothing," I said, jokingly. "Have your parents been contacted?"

"Yes......." She tried to say something else but couldn't quite form the words. I was touched by her defenseless situation and wanted to protect her. She tried to speak again. "Will you stay in the flat for me whilst I'm away.....It's so easy to break into. I'd feel so much better knowing you were there." She let her head relax and closed her eyes. How could I refuse her? As she lay there, with hardly the strength to breath, I felt very concerned and apprehensive. I was moved to tears by the time I was leaving the hospital. This still didn't stop me from looking for Stuart's car. It was gone. Putting this to one side I returned to the flat as requested. On entering I looked around at all the familiar objects, the bookshelves, the sewing patterns, her dresses, shoes, they cried out a welcome. At this moment it felt good to be back, so I stayed.

Within three days Jenna remarkably recovered much of her previous strength and was sufficiently recovered to take short walks to the end of the ward and back. A few days later I brought Jenna home to her flat. She would need help for a few weeks yet and as far as she was concerned, I was the only one to help her and spoke convincingly of how much she needed me. At the same time Stuart was clearly around somewhere, just out of sight, no doubt waiting for the moments I disappeared. Yet with a surprising amount of coolness, she refused to even talk about it, which frustrated me. I clearly had no control or influence over this affair. It had been nearly three months since the fateful party, and I was already beginning to separate myself from this previous life. Natasha had helped do that. With Stuart still around I was reluctant to step back into it all again. I knew in my heart this was all over. Despite this I decided to stay in the flat, partly to see if it was really possible to regain any of the magic we had before and partly, because it was convenient. After all there was only one month to the end of term and hopefully starting a job.

I had applied for many jobs, but it seemed most likely I would succeed with the National Coal Board. I was just waiting for the letter of confirmation. However, each weekend I returned to play in the band with Brian. We now called the band Ashley Snow, a name conjured up by Brian. Quite why, I never really understood. Whilst Jenna and I were together Brian was never a major advocate of her, he thought Jenna a little snooty. Nevertheless, Brian raised his eyebrows in disapproval on the occasions he saw me with Natasha. "This isn't fair Nick." He would say in a wise and thoughtful voice. "It's bound to cause trouble." He was genuinely concerned. I knew he was right but I rationalised, if I join the NCB I will be leaving within a week or two.

As the day drew nearer attempts at signalling the inevitable just aroused anxiety. "Where was I going to stay? How was she going to see me? By not answering just created more anguish. I would telephone Natasha and tell her of the dilemma. She was still only a new friend and I suspected she had a personal agenda of her own during the week. I hadn't really asked such personal questions as yet. It was early days and arrangements were wonderfully relaxed.

All this changed, however, one dark evening whilst arriving back at the flat. Just before I entered my attention was drawn to a parked car as the headlights repeatedly flashed. It was Natasha. She had driven to Birmingham on the off chance of seeing me for a couple of hours. I was flattered by the attention. No girl had shown this kind of attention before. For the first time it seemed I might be the focus of Natasha's attention. I was drawing strength from this attention; it would make the break-up with Jenna that much easier.

I made my excuses to Jenna, telling her I needed to play the piano. She appeared to accept the story. On my return, however, I felt very guilty. I sat at the edge of the bed, feeling agitated, trying hard not to show any of my inner thoughts.

"Nick," said Jenna, signalling my attention, "I know we have our problems but do you think we could stay together?"

"I don't know." This wasn't very reassuring.

"When you get a job will you still want to see me?"

Looking up I could see the same Jenna I'd fell for at the very first dance. The light in the room gently illuminated the soft features of her face I was touched by the gentle tone she used. I wanted to comfort her. Yet she wasn't innocent.

"Brian and Mavis have invited us to go and stay next month for the weekend." I tried not to reply since the reality was; I expected to have left by then.

"You are coming, aren't you?" she said more insistently.

"I suppose so," There was a vagueness attached to my tone.

"I've got some good ideas for a holiday this year....." began Jenna.

I had to change this subject. It was too painful to continue with this. "Tracy and Craig have booked a villa in Italy and they're looking for someone to share. It sounds like a good idea doesn't it.?" Jenna was trying her best to pin me down.

"I'm just going to play my guitar," I said suddenly. It was too sudden.

"Just after playing the piano!" said Jenna in disgust. "Oh no you're not."
I picked up the guitar anyway, whilst I tried to think of another excuse.

 "You're not playing that guitar now." She said again

emphatically and then came over to take it away from me. Her voice was so assertive it irritated. I stubbornly held on to it.

"Look, you don't really want to play," she said again in a determined way and then began unbuttoning her blouse.

"Not tonight Josephine," I responded bluntly. Having just come from Natasha I just couldn't carry on with this.

"But I know you want to," she said insistently. The voice was not at all affectionate, only determined.

"Oh no I don't," I replied with equal insistence. I took a tight hold of my guitar as she tried to move it to one side. "Look, I don't want to," I said trying to sound authoritative.

She took up a position behind me and began to undo my shirt buttons, trying to lift up my shirt. I resisted. I was not going to give in. She took off her blouse entirely and undid her bra. She then began to press and caress her breasts against the back of my neck. Her movements became more and more erotic. I began to yield. My resistance was weakening. She reached forward to take my hand and placed it on her breast. It felt so difficult to resist.

"Did Stuart come to visit you in hospital?" I asked pointedly. She froze for a moment and then tried to pull the guitar out of my other hand. I was unyielding. She then tried to kiss me. "Did Stuart come to see you at the hospital?" I repeated.

"Why do you ask?" she replied cautiously.

"You know why I ask," waiting to hear what kind of approach she would decide to take.

"I wish you wouldn't talk about him. It's so unnecessary. I want you. I want you so much," she said firmly, "Kiss me."

"No, answer me," trying to hold her off. She tried again to kiss me, but I resisted. Then she tried to pull me down onto the bed, but I wouldn't move. I let go of the guitar and tried to stand up, but Jenna was in virtual fighting mood. I wrestled to get free, but I couldn't, not without actually hurting her. In silence we continued to scuffle. Jenna was trying to laugh but it was forced, and I was getting tired and irritated.

"Let me go," I demanded.

"Not until you give me a kiss,"

I was not going to give in. I began to apply more force to escape and as I did, Jenna began to dig in her nails. I felt the pain in my chest and stomach. I tried again to break free, her nails continuing to rip against my flesh. Finally, she let go and I could see the blood had stained my shirt. Without speaking I went to the bathroom to inspect the damage and clean up. That night I slept on the floor.

The next day came a letter of acceptance from the NCB, asking me to join a team of geologists at their Opencast Division in Nottingham. With great relief I announced to Jenna I would be moving out immediately to find a flat in Nottingham. What I couldn't understand was that although I was leaving abruptly, escaping the insufferable atmosphere we had generated, there was still a residual feeling of not wishing to leave. As I packed my bags into the car I still wanted to hold her. I wanted it so much to be right. Jenna watched me close the car door and then said tearfully.

"When will I see you again?" I looked up thoughtfully.

"I'll call you." She left it at that, and I drove away. I was sad and almost wished another argument had ensued, just to have been delayed a little longer.

I drove straight to Nottingham and, via a house agent, found myself a depressing one roomed, self-contained bedsit in the suburbs, opposite a park but close to the office. My salary was one thousand, two hundred pounds per annum, only a little more than I previously received in my grant. I couldn't afford much better. The bedsit was on the first floor in a large Victorian house. I dumped my bags in the nearest corner, and then I sat on the edge of a rickety bed staring at four blank walls and the rain outside. The walls were papered in an unusual bluey pattern, torn and yellowed with age, and in one corner it was damp. The carpet was old and worn. It had a sink and drainer, a small stove, a pre-war dressing table, armchair and bed. Although shabby and cheap I had to accept that this was all I could realistically manage on my finances. Inevitably I eventually picked up the guitar to pass a bit of time. I began to experiment with a new sequence of chords and within a short time I had a new song.

"Long time ago, we had a love,
As fresh as the breeze, as bright as the sun,
But now that you're gone, look at the falling rain".

CHAPTER SEVEN

The next week was spent settling into my new job. This turned out to be a very brief experience due to being immediately transferred to a local office in Hucknall, situated just off the M1 between Sheffield and Nottingham. Although somewhat of a surprise, it was, in fact, only a short drive away, and so two hours later I was dispatched and standing outside a new place of employment. The so called office building, was a long prefabricated wooden structure sited inside the grounds of a colliery. I entered and found my way into the nearest large room. A few people were working and seemed to pay little attention to my intrusion. The room was very basically furnished, almost pre-war in appearance.

"Can I help you? said one of them finally.

"I'm looking for Bill Thompson," I replied nervously.

"I'm Bill Thompson," he said authoritatively. "What can we do you for?" he said jovially with a rich northern accent. Bill was tall, thin and dark haired with pointed features and a long nose. He seemed to have a sense of humour.

"I'm a new geologist from Nottingham. Am I in the right place?" I ventured.

"Well I don't know about that. It really depends on your philosophy in life," he joked and turned to see the reaction from the others. Obviously, he enjoyed having an audience.
"What's your name?" he asked.

I told him. He looked again at the others and then returned his glance to me.

"So, you're the new 'Doctor in the house,' said with an element of amusement. Somehow his tone now sounded patronising. "We've been waiting for you. We've never had this privilege before."

"What's the big deal?" I thought to myself. He looked around at the others. They didn't react.

"I suppose I should do the introductions." He continued, reluctantly, and then gestured towards a young lady sat at a drawing board at the side of the window.

"This is our geological artist, Yvonne. She changes all our incomprehensible scribbles into works of art." She had long blonde, bleached hair but petite attractive features. The way that she was smoking, however, suggested a tenseness. I hoped I was wrong.

"I'd just like to say that Bill's scribbles are the most challenging," added Yvonne. Bill ignored her and turned towards a dark haired, guy well built with a ruddy complexion.

"And this is Paul. He looks after the south Nottingham area." He was of a similar age to myself, and looked a little sullen as he sat at his desk. He didn't say anything and continued working. Bill looked finally over to the far end of the room.

"And of course, there is Eddie, recently promoted to curate all our working sites and develop a strategy of sales for outside bids." Eddie appeared easy going, tall slim with wiry neat hair and horn-rimmed spectacles. He smiled and seemed relaxed.

After this short introduction I was shown to my desk. It was by a large window and had the advantage a panoramic view of the Colliery and its surrounding countryside. I sat down and began to casually glance through some reports which already lay on my desk.

There was still one person I hadn't met and that was the boss, Keith. At the Nottingham office his reputation went before him. He was apparently keen and ambitious, and aiming for the top. He was already nominated to represent the Liberal Party in the up and coming election and was popular amongst the higher echelons of the NCB, where it mattered. So, when I was called to his office, I did just wonder what exactly I was going to meet. But as so often in these situations the reality is nearly always something else. Keith was courteous, charming and helpful. No hint of unreasonable expectations or unnecessary pressure. He sorted out a few introductory forms and then organised my work program for the first few days. It appeared I would spend half the day in the office and the other half out in the field pegging out drill holes for the drilling rig, monitoring the drilling and collecting the data. Not a mention about politics. All very smooth and amicable. I returned to my desk and started the process of filling out forms. There were several and none of them seemed straight forward. And so, I began. My very first job in the real world. It was a daunting thought.

After a few minutes came a welcome distraction. A young girl of about twenty one years, walked into the office carrying papers which she gave to Bill. Bill was still in a tormenting mood.

"Don't talk to me about those sort of things Ruby luv." He bellowed obviously. "Why not ask the new boy over there. You've not met him yet. Why not go and have a chat with him, I know you want to."

Ruby went bright red in the face as everyone's attention was drawn to see her reaction. Reluctantly she obediently walked across the room towards me. She had a plump portly figure but at the same time an immediately endearing quality about her. Clearly, she was feeling very awkward.

"Nice one Bill. We can always rely on you to embarrass," shouted Eddie.

As she came to a halt in front of me, she leaned over in an attempt not to be heard by Bill. "I need to find out if you're going to eat in the canteen....... for lunch...... or if you wish to make your own arrangements." Paul Needham, sitting only a few feet away overheard the vital few words.

"Hear that Bill," he said, quickly interrupting, "she's asking him out to dinner."

I could feel we were both being put on the spot for their amusement. Eddie kept his head down at the back of the room, whilst Yvonne sat back and waited for a reaction. Bill obliged.

"Well you know Ruby, she likes her food," he said with amusement and with a grin that showed all his teeth to the extent that they almost glowed.

"Thank you, for the invitation Ruby," I said to her, smiling, "I would be delighted to have lunch with you." She smiled back and put an appropriate mark on her papers. She turned to leave returning a cheesy grin to Bill as she left.

"Don't let Bill bother you," said Yvonne, swinging around on her chair, "he can't stop himself annoying people." She pushed on the desk and then skilfully completed one full revolution to return back to her drawing board. Bill continued.

"I don't have to annoy people, it's just that I enjoy it so much." He said it proudly, again filling the room with his shining teeth. I decided to concentrate on my work and returned to the forms I was trying to fill out.

Fortunately, it wasn't that long before the day ended, and it was time to make my way down the motorway to Nottingham. I had hoped to have arranged something for the evening ahead but for one reason or another, it hadn't happened. By the time I reached the bedsit I felt distinctly alone. As I parked the car and stared at the glum exterior of the place, I really felt a reluctance to enter. The stairway and corridor in the house did not communicate a desire to socialise. Such a contrast to the early college days when doors remained open inviting social contact. In the darkness of the corridor I fumbled for a light switch. The click yielded a yellow glow at the top of the stairs. I slowly ascended hoping I might coincidentally meet with one of the other tenants. Of course, I didn't and within minutes the door to my bedsit was closed and I was staring out of the window into the grey night. The bed was a mess, it needed changing. I opened a tin of soup and made some toast. I thought about Natasha. She was in Rotherham, a forty minute, drive away. I'd only made arrangements for the weekend but now wished I'd arranged something earlier. After eating I went to find a call box. The call box was smelly and the receiver sticky. At least it worked. I tried Natasha's number but there was no reply. I returned to the bedsit and retired early.

During the car journey to work the following day my thoughts continued to weave a network of endless circles about Jenna. I still longed for her and yet I hated her. Her relationship with Stuart simply tormented me. That it could still be going on, destroyed any chance of reconciliation. Somehow, I had to resign myself to the fact that a fundamental part of our relationship was destroyed. It was gone forever.

At the office Natasha phoned. She wanted me to meet her parents in Nottingham that evening. What a relief, at least I wouldn't be confined to barracks this evening. Fortunately, my mind would be fully occupied this morning with work out in the field, pegging out the well locations. Such a task doesn't, on first appearances sound very exciting. I suppose for most people it isn't. However, with a little help from the imagination I could change this simple act of sticking a few wooden pegs in the ground into an intriguing detective story of global proportions. Having always been fascinated with how the universe operates, these few drill holes would almost certainly provide new glimpses into this world. One just needs to know how to look.

Today, however, I would try to confine some of my thinking time to the specifics of the job. This required me to understand the probable layout of the coal seams some 50-100m below the surface, together with their quality and volumes. The proposed site was close to the village of Godkin and comprised an old, derelict coal mine and several fields in the surrounding area. Without being provided any further information about procedures I drove to the location and parked the car as near to the site as possible. I could see the drilling rig in the distance, already in location close to the edge of a field. It was a fine beautiful day so I had no problem climbing over a few fences, frightening a few cows and tramping along the long grass to where the rig was actually standing. I paused to sniff the air. It wasn't fresh. It was rich with the smell of pig manure. I pressed on. It was just good to be outside in the sunshine instead of the office. As I approached, I could work out more of the rig's structure. It was actually quite a simple apparatus, essentially consisting of a lorry with a drill tower on the back. One of the drilling crew spotted me and came over.

"I'm Harry, drill supervisor," he announced, shouting to make himself heard. "Wait a minute I'll switch off."

He returned to the rig and a few seconds later peace was restored to the countryside. The other two crew members watched on blankly as they stood in a pool of mud that surrounded the rig. Their clothes were almost covered in mud.

"I see you get a bit dirty doing this sort of work?"

"Aye, just a bit. So, you're new then?"

"Uh huh." I grunted, anticipating further comment. "You'll have to bear with me whilst I find my feet," I warned.

"I'll help you along if I can.......We're almost finished in this field as you can see, so I'll need you to peg out the next one as soon as you can." He pointed over a hedge and so I cross checked with my map for any underground service pipes or cables. One of the things that you certainly had to avoid.

"You ought to go and see the farmer and make sure it's alright if we use that opening in the hedge over there to drive the rig through."

I agreed and set off towards the farm. I could see the farm buildings. They were not far away on the other side of an adjacent ploughed field. I began my approach along a well-trodden footpath. It wasn't long, however, before I noticed that the field had just been recently covered in highly volatile pig manure. The intensity was so high that I found myself gasping for oxygen. There was so little of it I could barely breathe. I walked faster. Within seconds I was running, still desperate for fresh air. It was with great relief when I eventually reached the other side and took a long lingering and delightful breath of clean air. I leaned against the fence and looked accusingly at the field.

"No sense in threatening the field," I mused.

The farmhouse now stood before me. The farmer was surprisingly cooperative, so it was a quick discussion. He had no problem with what the drillers wanted; no doubt because he knew he would be compensated handsomely for any damages. I took the long way back, steering clear of the problem field.

It was time to set about pegging. The field was nice and grassy without any nasty smells. Within an hour I was finished. In the corner of the field were laid out several long narrow boxes with cores of rock and coal which had been cut by the drill rig. This was another part of the job description. I had to describe in detail and sample these cores. I walked over to them, avoiding the menacing glances of a cow as it was obliged to move out of the way. There was a lot to do. I fumbled for my book and searched everywhere for a pen. After a thorough search of my pockets it appeared by luck, hiding in the lining of my coat pocket. Now I was fully armed, there was no alternative but to start. I began at the far end, kneeling down and squinting hard at the murky blackness of the coals. I could see the subtle changes that indicated the different parts of the swampy primeval forest that existed here at this time. I became engrossed, looking up only to take in the beautiful green of the surrounding fields, a single tree majestically swaying against an almost clear blue sky and the occasional sound of cows munching coal. It was the realisation of this last point that made me suddenly turn around. Several cows were tucking into a mid-morning snack, noses buried deep into the boxes, eating wholesale portions of this obviously prime tasting Barnsley Coal Seam. I blinked twice in disbelief.

"Clear off!" I shouted. "Stupid cows, clear off!" I repeated. They begrudgingly began to move away. But not far, they wanted more. "What to do now?" Several of the coals had been decimated with virtually nothing left of them. My first week, what a start. I chased the cows as far away as I could and then went to find Harry. He didn't seem at all surprised and gave me a hammer and nails to close up the remaining boxes. We arranged the re-drill of the worst affected cores. As we stood in discussion the rig suddenly started to shudder in front of us, and lurch forward, as the pipe string appeared to drop down into the well hole. Harry immediately stopped the rig rotary motor.

"Stand away now," he commanded to his workmates. "Well back," he insisted. "You too, Mr. Townsend." He looked concerned. "No smoking!" he shouted to one of the crew. I watched him as he sniffed the air and stared at the hole. He seemed to be waiting for something and listening all the time. He waited another minute and then sniffed the air again. The rest of us stood at the edge of the field. Harry eventually moved closer to the rig and got a hold of the drill pipe. It seemed to move easily as though hanging free. He let it go and then came over to us.

"We'll have to leave it for an hour. Can't do anything for the moment," he said almost apologetically.

"What is it?" I asked him.

"Gone into a large underground cavity, probably Roman,"

he said with an air of resignation, "these shallow coals were often already mined by the Romans and every now and then we drill into one. There is just an open cavern down there. It sends the rig forward like this. "The problem is these cavities are filled with bog gas, which is mainly methane, and is highly inflammable and although you can't see it, it is actually pouring out of that hole right now. Any spark and the whole thing could go up like a rocket."

I listened earnestly. "How do you know when it is safe again?"

"When the pressure has been entirely released it's relatively harmless, but I always leave it an hour to be sure. We once drilled and found a Second World War bomb. Amazing what you find down there." He finished his stories and so I left reassured. But not for long as I suddenly remembered the cores.

"Oh no, the cows!" I groaned. I turned and rushed back towards the adjacent field. Hopeful but not optimistic I approached the group of cows clustered around the boxes. The sight of me running, arms and legs flailing, did not immediately deter their appetite. Only when I reached the boxes did the last cow move away revealing the disaster area. How was I going to explain this back at the office? All these well locations would have to be cored again. I felt a mild depression descending over me as I attempted to nail down the lids. Sooner or later I would have to report back to the office. This was a steep learning curve. There was obviously a lot more to this job than placing pegs.

An hour later I was standing outside Keith's office searching for some words of explanation. Before I could I knock, Bill appeared and beckoned me down the corridor. Somehow his expression seemed ominous. "They know already," I cursed and then braced myself.

"What's been going on, Nick?" snarled Bill, "Keith is really on the warpath." Curiously, he didn't smirk as I expected. His expression remained concerned. Head down, I sighed and then took a deep breath.

"How was I to know that cows eat coal," I blurted out in exasperation.

"What are you talking about?" he retorted, "The farmer's pigs and the sheep dog are dead." He retained an angry expression. "They suffocated and died in the bog gas you released." He said it with venom in his voice but yet a look of smugness in his face. I could see Paul suppress a snigger and then hide his head behind the drawing board. Yvonne looked over with a little more sympathy. "It was your responsibility," he continued.

"My responsibility!!" I screeched, "How was I to know?" I suggested looking around for some signs of support.

Eddie interceded. "It is usual practice to inform the farmer if there is likely to be a risk of methane seepage. When it escapes, it collects and concentrates in hollows. The weather being good today, the gas would have collected in the hollow where the pigsty is and the dog was snoozing. I think you were just unlucky to have been caught out like this in your first week"

"Nevertheless, it was your responsibility," interrupted Bill. My body began to tingle and then melt like jelly. Bill watched my discomfort with a sense of satisfaction and then suddenly remembering what I had said earlier began again, "Anyway, what's this you were mumbling about cows? Have you killed them as well?" he scowled. I didn't answer and went to sit down at my desk. I desperately looked for something to do to take my attention away from them. Yvonne looked up from her drawing board and glanced slowly around the room, her nose twitching.

"What's that smell?" she asked with a pained expression. Suddenly she coughed. "Ugh. It's awful. It smells like manure!" I left the room in a hurry. As I shut the office door I could hear Yvonne say, "It's Nick. I'm sure it's Nick."

Again, I found myself outside Keith's office still searching for something I could use for a defense. "It's now or never," I muttered and then knocked. I knocked again, there was no answer. He wasn't in. I wandered slowly down the corridor reluctant to go back in our office. Almost aimlessly I passed by Ruby's office thinking there might be a more friendly reception in there. I could see her, but hesitated, remembering the 'odour de cochon' emanating from me everywhere I went. Instead I went to the toilet to try and clean up a little. It would appear the only sanctuary left for me. I stood and stared at myself in the mirror. I looked worried. I rinsed myself under the tap. It felt better. Outside, I heard the sound of people leaving. It was 5.45pm. I gave myself one more rinse, dried off, and then stepped back out into the corridor. In our office only Eddie remained. He was preparing to leave.

"You do realise that they're a little jealous of your Ph.D. ....They don't like a 'Doctor in the house'," he said as I walked in. "They want to see you knocked down." He continued. I stared at him in surprise that one of them could actually say anything remotely friendly. "But more than that, Bill as senior geologist, was actually responsible for informing you about methane procedures and the other problems you endured. And as far as I can tell, you were not told. It's Bill who will ultimately suffer, not you. He wanted to see you fall but it's going to backfire on him.

That's why he's behaving so badly." He didn't wait for a response. He turned and left.

I left the office in sombre mood. Tired, depressed and worried I made my way out to the car. It stood alone, the only remaining vehicle in the car park. I was now supposed to meet Natasha's parents for the first time. Not the best of times. I opened the car door and slumped into the driver's seat. I had suffered today. Not tragically, but nevertheless it was pain. Despite the many events of the day, the tone of Bill's voice remained uppermost in my mind. He was determined to exploit the situation. But why so venomously? As I managed to start the engine I began to think if the suffering was really necessary. Like everybody else in this world I prefer to avoid suffering where possible. It seemed ironic that despite all the criticism, that none of it really had much to do with the poor pigs and the dog.

"Are you alright?" came a voice from the other side of the car, "Do you need help?" It was one of the miners on his way home. He gave me a strange look. I felt embarrassed. I continued to sit there a short while until he disappeared out of sight. At least I'd put Bill out of my mind for a few minutes.

I reversed the car and steered it along the high mountainous wall of slag heaps that adorned the main entrance area. Such scenery formed an ugly eyesore to most people, but I had grown up in such surroundings and found it strangely reassuring and comforting in its ugly splendour. I drove on towards the outskirts of Nottingham and the address I had been given for Natasha's parents. I knew the approximate location. I just needed to search out the precise house. I arrived on time, but with no time to change.

The house was detached with large bay windows and an ornate archway over the front door. It was situated along a busy main road leading into Nottingham, so busy, in fact, I drove past it twice unable to slow down sufficiently to make a turn in to the drive. The land rose steeply away from the road, the house standing high, along with several others. I turned the car into the narrow steep drive and stopped. I was now marooned at a 45degree angle. I had no choice other than to park so I pulled the handbrake as far back as it would and pushed the gear stick firmly into first. At this angle I just hoped it was secure. As I switched off the lights I could see Natasha at the front door. She warmly greeted me but then looked disapprovingly at my office clothes. "It's no good her grimacing," I thought, "This is all I have in the world." My discomfort became more acute as I suddenly realised the absence of a gift.

"Is there a shop open anywhere?" I asked, before stepping in. "I haven't brought anything." I felt disorganised and thoughtless.

"Oh, don't worry about that," she said calmly, "I've told them we are going out. Just come in and say hello."

I felt relieved and stepped in. The hallway was lined with an unusual mixture of objects pushed chaotically along the edges of the walls. Plastic bags, shoes, a bicycle, coats and two vacuum cleaners. I looked for a place to put my coat. There wasn't. I held on to it and followed Natasha into the living room. The room also had a similar appearance. Her father stood up immediately to firmly shake my hand. It was direct but friendly. I immediately liked him. He was very tall, balding with blonde receding hair and a neat moustache. Her mother remained in her chair in a snoozing position, eyes flickering, barely open and loosely holding a pair of knitting needles. She wore a dark brown cardigan over a tight, black polo neck jumper. A trail of cigarette ash was conspicuous as it lay on her lap. As though requiring considerable effort, she opened her eyes and began a series of slightly exaggerated movements to sit herself up and take notice what was going on.

"Oh Nathan, why didn't you tell me we had visitors," she said with what seemed forced surprise. I introduced myself. She remained seated.

"Oh, hello," she said, her words almost taking on a regal tone. She blinked in an obvious manner as though to confirm the body language of surprise.

"Nathan could you get me a cup tea." She made herself comfortable. Nathan got up and picked up the tea pot that sat on a pile of used newspapers and magazines which themselves masked a tea trolley underneath. He tested the weight of the teapot.

"I think you'll have to make a fresh pot," she said disappointedly, ushering him into the kitchen. Natasha returned to the room.

"I've got my coat. Are you ready to go?"

Her blonde hair curved attractively around her face as she smiled at me enthusiastically. I always found these first glances of Natasha very enticing. She had an immediate attraction difficult to quantify. Before I could answer, her mother interrupted.

"Have you time for one cup of tea before you go? Nathan's just about to make one." I looked over to Natasha for some clues. "After all Nick's only just arrived and you're whisking him off.......Going drinking are you?"

That last remark had a certain edge to it, I said to myself. I followed Natasha's grimaced expression and declined the invitation. We left by the front door again striding over a plastic bag on the way. Amazingly the car was still in place clinging for its dear life on the mountain slope. We made a hesitant reverse operation out of the drive into the fast moving, traffic and headed for a nearby pub about five miles down the road. The pub was very full and had to fight my way to the bar to get some drinks. As I tried to attract the barman's attention I glanced back towards Natasha. She was talking to a young lady. They obviously knew each other. I watched them briefly as they spoke eagerly to each other. My turn finally came to be served. I ordered a pint of bitter and Natasha's request, a brandy and babycham. I turned to fight my way back. The young lady had gone.

"Who was that?" I asked with curiosity.

"Who?" she parried.

"The young lady you were just talking to."

"No one."

"You were talking very busily to no one."

"What did you think of my parents?" changing the subject. We began to discuss them at length. She began to criticize her mother and generally praise her father. Since this fitted with my first impression there were no areas of immediate conflict. The evening's conversation went by easily and the traumas at the office seemed to melt away.

"Have you heard from Jenna?"

"No," I replied assuredly.

"I do feel sorry for her, you know," she began, "how could you leave her like that."

I was taken aback by this concern.

"Are you going to leave me like that as well?" she asked pointedly.

"No, of course not," I said firmly. "But I'm sure I'll think of something," I added jokingly. "Anyway, it will be you getting rid of me, I'm sure." There was a pause.

"Does this mean what I think it means?" I said with curiosity.

"What do you mean?" she asked.

"That you and I..... that we are ...er...going out?" I said clumsily, "you know...together."

"I think you know that already, without me telling you," she said reassuringly, and then reached across to touch my hand.

"How long had you been going out with Jenna?" she asked, again returning to this same issue.

"Oh, I don't know," I said vaguely.

"About four years, wasn't it?" she continued.

"I'm not pleased how things turned out. It all got too difficult," I said defensively.
"Surely you miss her after all that time. She looked so pretty in her photograph?" The subject was becoming strained. "I would like to meet her sometime, to explain what happened." I decided it was time to go and so we

drove back to her parent's house. Natasha invited me in for a coffee, but I was genuinely tired and realising the day ahead of me tomorrow, I made my excuses and left.

Back at the bedsit, the dowdy drab room was waiting for me. I consoled myself with the fact I had no need of luxurious surroundings and the little I spent on the bedsit saved me going overdrawn at the bank. I cheered myself up by finding some fresh bed linen in my bag that my mother had packed. I remade the bed, brushed my teeth, then switched off the light and got in. The welcoming feel of the cool, clean, fresh sheets was a delight. I took one last look at the room lit by the yellow streetlight. It made a hideous design on the already ghastly pattern of the wallpaper. I went to sleep listening to the drumbeat of the water pipes as they knocked repeatedly against the walls each time a tap was used. I must have been asleep only a few minutes when suddenly I was awake again. A loud persistent knock at my door echoed menacingly through the house.

"Let me in Nick!" came a voice, "please let me in........It's me." I was still drowsy but nevertheless recognised the voice. It was Jenna. I got up and opened the door. She was still making a lot of noise.

"Keep your voice down," I said in a hushed voice. As she let herself in, I noticed a door opening and the irritated look of one of the other tenants. I turned away and closed my door.

"What are you doing here, for heaven's sake?" I said irritated. "And keep your voice down," She continued loudly and with a piercing quality.

"Oh Nick, I've had an awful journey.....I just had to come and see you.....I just had to."

"How did you know I was here?" I asked with indignant surprise. She side glanced my expression and began again.

"You won't turn me away will you......I couldn't go back tonight, I need you." Her voice was like that of a lost soul in an amateur dramatics play.

"Be quiet!" I urged. Then realising what she was leading up to, "You mean you want to stay here the night!" I said more irritated.

"Just tonight, I'll go in the morning, ...I promise,.....I just needed to see you, to talk to you......Please Nick......Don't throw me out." Her voice was becoming more plaintive but yet insistent. In fact, I sensed nothing would persuade her to leave. She would just make more noise and get us both thrown out. I was also becoming aware of the limited range of sleeping options. They comprised the bed, the chair or floor. It seemed like game, set and match to Jenna.

"I don't like this," I said grumpily and climbed back into bed. "It's no good you staying...... I have a new girlfriend now." I spoke quickly without thinking, shocked that I'd actually said it. I awaited her reaction. Without comment she took off her coat and then continued further to undress until she was wearing only her underwear. Strangely she said nothing about this new information.

"You're going to be cold on the floor dressed like that,"

"I need to be with you," she said intently trying to make a space for herself in the bed.
I gave up and turned over, presenting a pair of cold shoulders to her. Tears began to fall from her eyes and roll down my neck. She sobbed uncontrollably and with a sense of desperation in each tear.

"Where do I go from here?" she whimpered. "I can't give myself like this to anybody else......I just can't.....only you....don't you see." I listened. I didn't know what to believe anymore. I could feel myself almost ready to give in. At the same time, however, there was an element of melodrama about all this and no matter what she said, the image of Stuart and Jenna at the flat always returned like an icy wind to remind me.

"Go to sleep," I murmured. "Promise you will be gone in the morning," I said coldly. She didn't answer, and so we went to sleep. The next morning, after the briefest of breakfast, I left for the office.

Trying to put everything behind me I entered the office as anonymously as possible. No one spoke as I walked towards my desk. The silence made it difficult to concentrate. I shuffled a few papers on the desk and attempted to ignore what seemed to me a heavy atmosphere. The phone rang shattering the silence. There was only one telephone in the office, and it stood on a table by Yvonne's drawing board. Yvonne answered. There was a pause as she listened.

"It's for you," she said without emotion. It was only 9.05am. I felt awkward as I moved to pick up the receiver.

"Nick Townsend," I said pensively.

"It's me Natasha, can I talk to you?"

"Ok. It's a bit early," I said quietly, "I'm a little busy at the moment."

"Can I see you tonight?" I thought for a brief moment, realising the implications. Jenna might still be at the bedsit.

"It could be awkward, you see." This was hopeless. I could sense everyone's ears burning in the room. Yet I had to tell her something. All this mystery was bothersome. "Jenna came around unannounced last night," There was a distinct pause.

"I'm coming round tonight," Her voice was determined. "I want to meet her." The phone went dead. I placed the receiver down.

"Somebody's pig died?" asked Bill sarcastically. The others laughed.

I returned to my seat to ponder the consequences. I still had to await the consequences of the methane incident. I was expecting a call anytime. The day dragged on, waiting and watching, wondering if I would be asked in to see Keith. It didn't happen and judging by the few words I had with Keith during the day, the incident had been contained. As I drove back to the bedsit that evening, I felt relieved, but not for long. Jenna's car was still parked outside. I went straight upstairs to find her trying to cook a meal on the single hob stove.

"You shouldn't be here," I said coldly.

"I've made you a meal."

"Natasha's coming round, she wants to meet you." She looked startled.

"Silly cow. The last thing I want to do is to meet her,"
"Then you had better leave," I demanded.

"Not until you've eaten this," she said insistently. "You're going to miss my cooking."

"We'll see."

To get her to leave without incident was not going to be easy. We ate together, whilst I tried to think of something.

"Why don't we go to the pub?" I suggested. She agreed. "I'll leave a note as to where to find us."

"Why bother!" she said angrily.

Being early, the pub was not very busy. We sat away from the bar to drink our halves of lager. The conversation was icy. Within minutes Natasha appeared. She came directly over to the table and sat down next to Jenna. Jenna gave her a disapproving stare as she moved closer to me and grabbed my arm.

"Aren't you going to introduce me?" asked Natasha and then reached over to take her hand. This startled me. Jenna, who didn't appreciate the contact, sharply withdrew her hand.

"What do you want?" Jenna asked indignantly.

"I want Nick to get me a lager...Or will you make it a brandy and babycham?" said Natasha in a sultry voice.

I felt uneasy, and with a sense of relief, went to the bar. I didn't understand the game being played here. All I wanted was to get back to the bedsit without a scene, and preferably without Jenna.

"Thank you, Nick," said Natasha as I returned. Jenna grimaced. They sat in silence a few moments, then Natasha spoke again

"She's very pretty Nick....She's got lovely fine blonde hair."

Jenna refused to look at her and turned to stare directly at me.

"Are you going to give me up for someone who talks like this?" interrupted Jenna.

Natasha appeared to move, either intentionally or unintentionally, closer towards Jenna. "Look!" said Jenna in almost astonished disbelief, "she's trying to touch me up."

"Look," I said quickly, "she's trying to talk civilly to you....Why do you have to make everything a confrontation," I said in exasperation. "Look, this meeting serves no purpose; I think you ought to go now."

"You want ME to go!" Jenna cried in disbelief, "but why?" Her voice although angry was becoming distressed. "Why Nick, Why?" As she said these words, she picked up her bag and made her way out.

"By the way.....does she know you slept with me last night?" Jenna said it with satisfaction. As though she always knew it was her ace card to play any time she wanted. And now she was using all the ammunition available. The statement hung in the air as I waited for a reaction. Jenna was gone and I was left alone with Natasha. Natasha's expression said it all.

"I knew she had come round last night. I hadn't realised you had slept together," she said quietly. I didn't add anything. What could I say? We sat in silence for a few minutes. Suddenly she got up and said.

"I'm going to get us some more drinks."

Natasha and I stayed on at the pub for a while longer.

Despite the previous tension, the remaining part of the evening went well as we began to put some of the events behind us, and even discussed some of the difficult issues that presently plagued me. The absence of confrontation in her approach was so refreshing and provided such a welcome contrast. One thing in all of this situation was clear, Natasha had a truly feminine appearance that spoke to me in a way that was difficult to resist. Not only that, but her mannerisms and conversation were always sensual which made her compulsive company. As the evening came to a close, we held each other close and then made our way back to the bedsit. Instead of returning to her flat Natasha decided to stay over.

The next day started calmly as we both left for work together. At the office I prepared myself for another day out in the field. The phone rang ominously at 9.30am. Yvonne answered. There seemed an interminable pause.

"It's for you," said Yvonne with a heavy sigh. She gave me a knowing look. The ears of the office tuned in again as I took hold of the receiver. It was Jenna. She sounded tearful.

"Nick, you can't do this to me, you can't leave me like this. I feel so alone...." The words seemed to go on without end and with no way of stopping them. The tone was agonising. With so many listening to my every word, however, I was compromised as to what I could say. Even though she was still talking I engineered an imaginary conversation.

"That would seem to be best.....So shall we leave it at that....Fine....Bye for now," I said over Jenna's voice and then put the phone down. I could see Bill sneer as I returned to my desk. I decided this would be a good time to visit the site, so I picked up my field bags and left the office. The periods on site were fast becoming my only refuge. It was a fine day and I enjoyed a moment to my own thoughts. This apparent calm lasted only until mid-afternoon when I returned to the office. I was greeted by Yvonne.

"She's rang again," she said anxiously, "several times!"

"I cannot see the attraction." Bill's despairing look said it all.

"She seems very upset." Yvonne was concerned.

"Oh dear, I'm really sorry about this......with their being only one phone.....And I simply can't stop her." I sat down to think of what to do next. "Was there any specific message?"

"Not that I could repeat here." Yvonne was trying to be tactful.

"How can you have so much trouble with women at your age?" interrupted Bill scathingly.

As I pondered further on the matter, I turned my gaze to the view immediately outside the window. I noticed a figure walking across the carpark. My heart sank, it was Jenna. At first, I refused to acknowledge I had noticed anything. However, it wasn't long before Bill spotted her.

"Nick," he began, "There's a girl stood out there and she's staring directly at you." Sure enough, Jenna stood about fifteen feet away from the window, her gaze fixed straight at me. "I don't think she's going to go away." He could barely contain his laughter.

"I can see that," I was annoyed. I decided to go out and

see what I could do. In full view of the staring eyes from the office window I made my approach. She stood there looking slightly coy. I stopped a few feet away from her.

"What do you want?.......Why are you here?" I asked with an irritated tone.

"I've come to say I love you and I want you back." She spoke softly and tried to reach out for my hand. I could still feel the eyes boring into the back of my head. I stepped back.

"Look this is embarrassing." I was struggling for something poignant to say. "I've made my decision and now I want you to leave me alone."

"But why Nick, why?" she said raising her voice. Her manner was becoming agitated.

"You know why," I said irritably, "Are you still seeing him?" I awaited her response.

"But I want you....he's not you." Her words deliberately steered away from saying a simple 'No'.

"Well you've got him now," I said pointedly, "so stop bothering me."

"You can't prefer that trollop!" Her tone much harsher now.

"Well if that's what you think, then at least she's my trollop."

"But she's weird."

"What do mean weird?" I replied indignantly, "What do

you call this present situation, then?" I said with further indignation. "This is what I call weird!"
I looked over at the office. "Anyway, this is getting us nowhere, *as always*, so please will you just go."

At last she turned, as if to go. "We had so much going for us.... we still do," She was whimpering now. "I'm not going to let her have you!" And with that she finally did walk away. Her car, a blue Hillman Imp, I could see parked some twenty yards away. I returned to the office. As I entered the main corridor I met Ruby. She had a sympathetic smile, so I stopped to talk a moment before entering back into the lion's den.

"Was that your girlfriend?" Her voice was soft and welcoming.

"It used to be."

"Oh dear." She spoke with concern.

"Has she just finished with you?"

"Something like that," I replied, realising at least she didn't seem to be aware of the entire story. I wanted to steer the conversation away from me.

"Who's your boyfriend?" Trying to be playful.

"Oooh, I haven't got a boyfriend." Her reply was awkward. I sensed I might have unintentionally embarrassed her.
"I didn't mean to pry." I quickly followed.

"Oh, it doesn't matter you asking," she said reassuringly with a smile. Just at that moment Bill stepped out of the office and observed us chatting. This brought a glint to his eye.

"Well, well," he began, "you just cannot stop yourself, can you Doctor Townsend. I'd be very wary of him Ruby.......He's dangerous." Bill grinned knowingly and continued down the corridor.

"I don't take any notice of him," she said calmly and then returned to her office. I did the same. Without Bill in the office there was an easier atmosphere and so I was able to sit a little easier back at my desk. Yvonne looked over at me.

"Was she alright?"

"Yes, I think so." I tried to raise a smile.

"What are you going to do about her?" She sounded genuinely concerned. "She's becoming a menace." Eddie was at the back of the office, listening.

"There are women like that." He paused purposely, "And men of course," he added, looking over to appease Yvonne, "They will follow you around forever. They never seem to give up.......Can become a big problem."

"That is something I simply wouldn't do," said Yvonne firmly and then returned to her work.

The brief moment of friendly conversation seemed to end there suddenly, and the atmosphere changed. I picked up my mapping pen and began to work. When the day at the office finally ended, I stepped warily outside and scoured the row of parked cars for any signs of a Blue Hillman Imp. There was a sense of relief as I managed to drive out on to the motorway without incident.

Jenna was making my life a mess and me, a laughing stock. I was growing increasingly angry at that. As I drove my Mini Van through some of the narrow backstreets of Nottingham, my mind began to focus on the embarrassment I was now having to endure. Suddenly the car in front of me stopped sharply. I reacted slowly and was only just in time to come to a screeching halt a few inches from his rear bumper. A fire-engine had pulled out in front of him and then began to weave his way between the parked cars and slowly moving traffic. I briefly chastised myself for not concentrating on the road in front of me as I should have been. I shook my head, in an attempt to wake up, and then moved on slowly. The traffic was now being forced to make more space and so had to pull over. When I was finally allowed to turn into the top of my road, I couldn't fail to notice a second fire-engine, apparently parked opposite the bedsit. The road outside was wet with dirty water, choked with black mud trickling down the pavement and into the gullies. As I opened the car window the air had a distinctive smell of burnt wood. Firemen were mopping up and tidying away the hoses. A small group of people stood on the pavement opposite, staring at the activity. The windows were broken, and the wood charred. The brickwork outside was darkened around the window and a small hole was noticeable on the roof where a few slates were now missing. I was horrified at the sight. It looked almost certain that it was my bedsit that had been on fire. My heart started pounding as the full horror of the scene began to unfold.

Now trembling I pulled the car over to the side of the road and parked. My first instinct was to drive off as fast as possible, but almost drawn by the impending disaster I got out of the car and began to walk a few steps closer towards the bedsit to get a clearer view. The group of people were now dispersing. Whatever had happened was now over. But what had happened? What had I done to cause this?

Words ran at an excruciating rate through my mind. What mistake or absentmindedness had led to this? The various possibilities began to run through and torture my mind. But then I remembered, the cooking stove hadn't been used this morning; I only had cereal for breakfast. With only this to reassure me I took more and more nerve tingling strides closer. Only three people now stood outside the house in discussion, standing next to the large red fire-engine. One of them glanced towards me. His expression was stern and his gaze cold. It was the landlord and he recognised me.

"There's that hippy!" he roared. His tone was vicious and menacing; his finger pointed accusingly straight at me. "There he is!" he roared again, mustering further resources of contempt. I felt my knees weaken. He was late middle age, wearing an old suit, distraught and demonstrating an unnerving ability to speak his own mind.

"He could eat me alive," I thought inwardly. In the short time I had to think, I rationalised my only chance was to sort this out whilst in the presence of others. Maybe they would have a restraining influence. I walked within arms each of the landlord.

"Smoking pot were you?" he said, clenching his teeth. "Drug party was it?" Now spoken with venom. He then turned to involve the others more directly. "Different girl every night, you know......Lord knows what was really going on." he continued. "You're going to pay for this, you scumbag....Your sort,.... you're all scumbags, the dregs of the earth." The other two men watched, waiting for a moment to interrupt. The rage of this man and his insults must have turned me quite pale as I stood there motionless.

"Are you Mr. Townsend?" said one of the men. He had a

dark plain uniform and was holding a notepad. I sensed he was connected to the Fire Department. His voice was sharp and clipped. I acknowledged him with a nod, not really daring to take my eyes off the landlord.

"Look Mr. Townsend, as you can see there has been a fire here this afternoon and obviously we need to find out what happened, and what you might know about it."

"You're dam right we're going to find out!" exclaimed the landlord, his hands held clasped together. "You can pack the remains of your belongings and get out," he hissed. "Go on, get out now!" he said with a strong pointing gesture. "Damn hippy." he muttered. The other man interceded at this stage.

"It might be better if we both go down to the police station and get a few statements down on paper. I'm the fire officer in charge and so would appreciate your cooperation in trying to obtain some more details surrounding this incident." Again, without a word I nodded. He then beckoned me down to a red Ford Escort. I followed and then got into the back seat. "It's not far," he said, breaking the silence. He then settled himself into the driver's seat.

"I don't know what could have happened." I was trying to offer my innocence.

"It seems the fire started in the bed. The bedding and sheets etc. all seemed piled up into a heap with letters and photographs circled around. It seems someone deliberately set it alite, almost like a ritual. That's why the landlord is convinced there is a connection with drugs." Despite the nature of this incident, the tone of his voice seemed calmer and more reassuring.

"I've never taken any form of drugs, ever, I don't even smoke." I protested.

"Does anyone else have a key to your room?"

"No." I replied without hesitation.

"A neighbouring tenant says he saw a girl entering into your room a few days ago," he added. I was struck by the serious possibility that Jenna had been responsible for all this mayhem. Despite an initial surge of anger at this thought, I decided to shape my response in such a way that wouldn't her involve her, for the time being.

"Yes," I confirmed, "I loaned her my key that day because she would arrive before I got back from work.....to save her waiting outside." I tried to make it sound innocent. This, however, was not true. I was growing more convinced she must have broken in. Perhaps because she suspected that Natasha had stayed the night. "At what time do you think the fire started?"

"About 4 o'clock," he answered thoughtfully. This was about one hour after Jenna had left me at the office. With this evidence, it seemed more likely than ever she did it.

"What's the name of this girl?"

"Ashley," I said nervously, "Ashley Wade." This was her middle name. "But I don't see how it could be her. We are more colleagues than anything else," I was again twisting the truth, trying to keep Jenna out of serious trouble. I couldn't really think why, except I had the vaguest feeling I could survive all of this provided it didn't get back to my parents. They couldn't take this, and I could suddenly picture Jenna's father and the landlord both turning up at my parents. The fire officer took out his notebook and wrote down her name.

"Do you have her address?"

"Sorry, I don't have it," I sounded unconvincing, "as I said, we are more like colleagues. She lives somewhere in the Birmingham area, I think."

"Could you find out?"

"I could try," I replied, trying to sound cooperative. He looked unconvinced, put away his notebook and took a firm hold of the wheel. We drove off in silence. The police station was only a short ride away and within a few minutes we were there.

"The police will want to ask you a few more questions," he said as we pulled up. I allowed myself to be escorted up the few steps to go inside. This was my first visit to a Police Station. We entered in through the main entrance, a classic Victorian frontage, and complete with an overhanging blue lamp. I was handed over to a constable, a small man who met us at the desk. He seemed distracted and unapproachable as the fire officer attempted to gain his attention. Eventually the constable conceded and made an effort to raise his eyes directly towards me.

"Is this the gentleman?" He then walked away, down the adjoining corridor and disappeared through a doorway. He returned together with a dishevelled looking younger man. After a brief discussion with the fire officer he then beckoned me to follow him. We went down the corridor and entered a small room where I watched him take his place behind a desk. The room had only the desk and two chairs and was very dimly lit. He shuffled a few papers and then looked up at me.

"Please take a seat," he said dryly and then proceeded to ask for further personal details which I gave. Satisfying himself of this introductory information he put down his pen and leaned back on his chair.

"The landlord believes you are taking drugs," His tone was stark. "Are you taking drugs?"

"No, certainly not," I rebuffed, "I've already said this, ...I don't even smoke." The half green painted wall around the room momentarily distracted me. It was wartime decor from another age, almost nineteenth century.

"How long have you been living at the bedsit?"

"About two and a half weeks, I've only been there a short time."

"And yet according to your landlord you appear to have had several female visitors all apparently desperate to see you; and yet you claim are only distant acquaintances," he said pointedly. "What is going on Mr. Townsend? ....Who set fire to your bed?" His voice was growing louder.

"I don't know," I said weakly.

"I think you do know, Mr. Townsend, and I think you know why." He looked as though he was about to say more when he paused and reached into one of the drawers in his desk. He pulled out a number of small sized, self-sealing plastic bags, the type I used on site for samples, and proceeded to spread them on the desk in front of him.

"What do you use these for?" His tone was demanding. I stared at them as they lay accusingly in front of me. This was staggering. How far was he prepared to take this ridiculous scenario?

"I'm a geologist working for the Coal Board. These are the bags I collect coal samples in for analysis." I said incredulously. I paused briefly and then decided to ask directly. "You're not seriously suggesting I keep drugs in these?" He was now writing and continued to write without answering. When he finished, he sat back and impassively asked, "Mr. Townsend, I ask you again. Who do you think started this fire and why?" He kept repeating my full name which seemed to add tension to the questions.

"I don't know. I'm totally bemused by the whole thing." Which I was. "I didn't know anything about the fire until I arrived back this evening."

The statements eventually came to an end and without further incident. But I revealed no more of Jenna's involvement. In fact, I had no real proof it was her. My main concern was that this investigation could lead to my parents becoming involved. I was very anxious to keep them out of it at all costs.

I left the Police Station and walked back towards the bedsit to collect my belongings, or what remained of them. There was little of real value, except I suddenly remembered my guitar. My pace quickened. As I turned the corner into the street to approach the bedsit, I slowed down again. The footpath leading to the house was soot stained and the black open hole of the broken window gaped down at me. I glanced around for signs of any prowling landlords. I entered. The hallway seemed in order, no obvious signs of damage. As I reached the top of the stairway, the door to my room lay open. A cold draft met my face, filled with dusty charred odours. I stepped inside. One side of the room was severely burnt. The metal frame of the bed lay exposed but covered with a thin layer of ash, but parts of the mattress and fragments of the sheets, together with letters, still remained. The wall against the window was black and damp from the work of the firemen. Hardly any curtains were left save for a few soddened and torn fragments strewn over the floor. The carpet was cratered with burnt areas. Worst of all was the ceiling which had suffered the most damaged. A large hole had been burnt destroying a part of the rafters. A small area of the roof slating had fallen through, leaving fragments of slate and burnt wood all over the floor. The cost of sorting all of this out would be enormous. At that moment I realised there would be more repercussions to come.

Miraculously my belongings, being concentrated on the other side of the room nearest the door had escaped. The old sideboard that contained my clothes and the few odds and ends, seemed intact. My guitar leaned against the sideboard and at first glance appeared unscathed. As I moved it, however, I could see on one side a small area that was blistered. Without ceremony, I collected my things and bundled them into the car. To my relief the landlord did not reappear. I suddenly felt tired as I started the car. The day's events had taken their toll. I turned my thoughts to going home. Perhaps there I could put this nightmare behind me for a while.

As I approached the familiar sights on the outskirts of Rotherham I stopped at a telephone kiosk to ring my parents. There was no answer. I decided to try Natasha; after all, she was virtually next door. Leaving out most of the day's details, such as fire engines and police stations, I succeeded in arranging to meet here at her flat. It was with great relief to finally park the car by the familiar sights of the flats. They seemed friendly and welcoming. Natasha came out to meet me and I began to explain a little of what had happened. I was glad to see her but yet slightly irritated by the excessive make up she wore and the garish colours of her clothes. I didn't comment. What did I know about fashion? There were still no signs of my parents. Undaunted I readily accepted an invitation to tea. Once inside I began to elaborate on the events of the day. Natasha appeared to be making the meal but not making much progress. Lisa, her flat mate was there, and listening intently to the story. Suddenly there was a knock at the door. Lisa giggled and shouted, "It's her, it's her!" Although she was joking, I think we all felt a degree of anxiety as she went to answer the door. It was a relief to hear my mother's voice. "It's your other woman," said Lisa sarcastically. I went to the door.

"Hello," announced mum chirpily. She seemed happy. Perhaps the bad news hadn't reached her. "I saw your car and wondered if you were going to call in."

"Yes, I'll be there in a minute." I was hoping not arouse suspicion. Natasha understood that I should leave and so after finishing a raw piece of carrot I made my way home. It was now nine o'clock. As I approached the flat, my stomach tightened to glimpse a blue Hillman Imp enter the grounds of the flats. Instinctively I stepped quickly into my parents' flat thinking I would be out of view. But then I realised my car stood like a beacon outside Natasha's flat. I said a brief hello to my parents but then went straight into the kitchen to look out for Jenna. Strangely there was no sign of her or her car. As I peered surreptitiously through the net curtains of the window, my mother entered the kitchen. She saw me and I could see immediately her suspicions were aroused.

"What's going on?" Her tone was serious, and stood there with folded arms.

"What do you mean?" Guilt must have been written all over my face. How much did she know?

"You know what I mean," Her voice that said it all, "Don't play games. I want to know."

"Jenna has been ringing here trying to reach you all day." "What's going on between you two?.......I thought you said you had finished with her a while ago." This time said with an irritated tone, "Are you leading her on? Messing her around? Because it looks like it to me."

"No mum, I'm not. At least I'm trying not to." I said defensively. If only she knew, I thought.

"But she sounds so upset and sobbing," obviously she was not convinced.

"You can't be seeing Natasha and Jenna at the same time. It's not fair," introducing a high moral tone.

"I've finished with Jenna but she keeps on following me....to work and things," I pleaded.

"Your father doesn't like it. Nicholas, you have got to stop leading girls on like this."

She went back into the living room. I would have to face my father next. My father stood for very little nonsense of this kind. He thought all problems could be solved with a clip behind the ear, and I could almost feel one coming on right now. Meanwhile, I was anxiously aware that Jenna could be out there right now about to appear at any moment. I had to go out there and somehow put a stop to all this; not least discuss the little matter of a fire. At least my parents didn't seem to know about that. I had to stop her. I gave another anxious look outside. There was nothing.

"I'm just going to see Brian and Philippa for two minutes.

Back in a minute," I shouted and then stepped outside. It was almost dark now and difficult to see if anyone was there or not. I looked up at the tall block of flats opposite where Philippa and Brian lived and to my surprise, I could see somebody waving from one of the windows. I continued to stare blankly for a moment until I suddenly realised it was Philippa. I waved back thinking it was coincidence. Philippa beckoned however, she was coming down. I shrugged my shoulders in an exaggerated manner and then waited. A minute later she reappeared at the base of the flats. I greeted her with enthusiasm. She gave little expression in return and beckoned me over.

"Guess who we've got upstairs!" she said dryly. "Jenna...She's inside." I groaned inwardly. "We're trying to persuade her to leave but she won't go without seeing you." I stood silently for a moment. I didn't want my parents or Natasha involved.

"Does she know I'm here?" I asked.

"She's not sure if you are with Natasha or your parents flat."

"I'm terribly sorry about all this. It's not your problem at all. I'll come up and see what I can do." We made our way up the stairs. No doubt my parents were already beginning to wonder where I was. As we arrived at the flat Brian was waiting at the door.
"She's in there." There was a benign look on his face. I didn't know what to say. This was all getting beyond the realms of mere embarrassment; completely new territory. He pointed into their bedroom where I could just see her sat on the edge of the bed, waiting. Brian shut the door behind me. Jenna stood up to approach me. She had a beige tweedy coat, tightly belted around her waist. Whatever state of mind she was in, she looked very smart.

She stood a few inches away from me and grabbed my arm, holding it firmly against her coat. I could now see the watery reflection in her eyes and the signs that she had been crying.

"What do you want?" I asked. "You're only causing trouble by coming here."

"Let's go somewhere else," she asked with insistence.

"You can." I said indignantly, "I'm staying here."

"Nick, I just want to be with you. I want to take off all my clothes and snuggle up in bed with you," She was now trying to lift out my shirt from my trousers.

"Did you start that fire?" I demanded whilst trying to hold down her arm.

"Yes!" she said sharply and without any signs of remorse. "You slept in that bed with that cow!......That bed was for you and me........" Her voice now trailed away as she broke into a sob. She tried to hug me but I refused the advance and pushed her away.

"Do you have any idea of the damage you caused, the danger you put people in?" I was angry. She continued to cry and more loudly.

"I know," she said pitifully. "I know I shouldn't have done it." Her voice now more remorseful. "I just couldn't help myself........The thought of you and her."

"Oh yes, and what about the thought of you and him?" I said sarcastically.

"It's not like that with him," spoken as though such a

statement was supposed to reassure me.

"Oh please Nick, let's go somewhere so we can do it," she demanded. "No one can give me an orgasm like you!"

I was taken aback by her boldness. Suddenly there was a knock on the door. It was Philippa. I turned to Jenna "Be quiet a moment."

"Nick, your father is at that door," said Philippa quietly. My heart sank again. Could this get any worse? "What shall I tell him?"

"I'll be out in a second," I whispered. I turned to Jenna. "Stay there and be quiet," I said forcefully and then stepped out of the room to speak to my father.

"Thanks Philippa." I then approached my father at the door. He looked pensive and angry at the same time.

"What's going on?" he demanded. "What are you doing?"

"Nothing, nothing at all. I'm just having a chat and I'll be down in a minute."

It sounded unconvincing. He glared at me. He knew something was wrong and continued to try and peer into the room behind me. Without another word he then turned to go. I was trembling. My father would never understand any of this. He would refuse to understand it and then almost unthinkingly put all the blame onto the nearest family member. In this case me. This was his usual procedure. But not without cost to himself. The torment of the disappointment he brought on himself, as a consequence, was also hard for him to take. Everything was black or white, good or bad. We were either perfect or useless, nothing in between. Usually the best anyone could achieve in the family was indifference. His demands could never be satisfied because, by default he had raised the standards too high. And yet despite this, he had a heart of gold, or should I say porcelain gold, that could be broken by a simple word out of place or a forgotten thank you. I think he knew this and, as a consequence, would always try to hide it and cope with his problems alone. So much so that we really hated to cause him any distress at all. It was as though no one was allowed to have a problem because it might upset father.

Brian and Philippa had been witness to this, and I was all out of excuses for the general public. I went back into the bedroom to find Jenna. She was sat looking very sorry for herself.

"Where's your car?" I demanded.

"It's behind here in the garages." She reached for her handkerchief. I took hold of her shoulders and steered her towards the door.

"It's over, isn't it Nick?" she said in her plaintive voice.

"Yes, you could definitely say that," I spoke without emotion. She blew her nose.

"It's really all over," she said again. The sound of each word seemed to stab at her in some sort of act of self-mutilation. She pulled away from me and quickened her step as she began to make her way down the stairs and out into the car park. I followed and watched her disappear behind the garages and then in seconds reappear in her car driving hard towards the exit of the grounds.

"There's going to be an accident." I muttered and then walked back to my parents flat. They were preparing for bed. I made another coffee in the kitchen hoping I could avoid another meeting with my father. My mother entered.

"Natasha called by, I told her you were up at Philippa and Brian's."

"Thanks," I said cautiously. Suddenly I realised I hadn't been back. I didn't even ask them how their plans for the wedding were progressing.

"We're off to bed now." I felt relieved. Trying to relax a little I drank the rest of my coffee. By the time my head reached the pillow I was really tired. The feeling of the cool fresh surface of the sheets against my face was so comforting after the struggles of the day. I welcomed the drowsy dream-like comforts that sleep had to offer.

Unfortunately, the next thing I remember was a knocking at the bedroom window. I stared at my watch. It was 4.30am. I leapt out of bed and stared out of the window. Jenna stood about five or six feet away beckoning me to go around to the front door to meet her. I should have gone straight back to bed. I wanted to. But I surmised in this situation Jenna would not probably want to give up and would then proceed to wake up the whole neighbourhood. I was still desperate to keep my parents out of this. Putting on a few clothes, I stepped quietly out into the hall to open the front door. She stood there motionless for a moment and then handed me a note. The writing was small and lay dense on the page and in the dim light I couldn't make it out.

"What's this for?" I asked in a hushed voice. I shivered and flung my arms around myself to keep warm.

"It's to say Goodbye." Then without ceremony handed me a small plastic bottle. It was empty.

"What's this?" I read the label on the bottle. "Sleeping pills?"

"I've just taken the whole bottle," she started to say proudly, but then a frightened look took over very quickly.

"You stupid girl!" I groaned exasperatedly. Checking for my car keys and closing the front door very quietly, I grabbed her arm and led her to my car. She came without protest and without comment. I was now wide awake. The hospital was only just down the road, less than five minutes away. I drove quickly. Fortunately, there was little traffic at this early hour of the morning. She sat quiet and still, at the side of me, her expression sad and pitiful.

"How long ago did you take these?"

"I've only just taken them," she said tearfully.

"How long is that?" I asked again irritated, "Five, ten, thirty minutes ago?"

"I don't know....five or ten minutes maybe."

The hospital was in sight and I pulled in off the empty roads towards the main entrance where a light showed some signs of activity. Leaving the car poorly parked we walked into the reception area. After little explanation a rather senior nurse in a dark blue uniform, guided us immediately to a doctor's office. Jenna was then unceremoniously dealt with. They spoke to her in angry severe tones emphasising the stupidity of the act. I was somewhat surprised by the cold unsympathetic approach they adopted, but at the same time I didn't blame them. I made myself scarce and disappeared to wait in the reception area. She was about to receive the ultimate punishment, the stomach pump.

At all times Jenna seemed alert and showing no signs of the drugs having taken effect. In fact, I was beginning to wonder if she had taken many, or even any, at all. "How many does one have to take?" I wondered. I waited nearly an hour. Outside I could see the grey light of the morning beginning to appear. It was almost 6.00am and I was the only person sat in the reception. I paced up and down a little longer until she finally reappeared accompanied by the doctor. Surprisingly there appeared to be few ill effects other than a stomachache and a bruised ego. Having thanked the staff for their trouble we stepped outside into the grey early morning mist. I gave Jenna a disparaging look.

"Shall I ring your parents?" Then rethinking I said, "No, you will ring your parents." She refused.

"They must know." I said.

"No, they mustn't know.... Please don't tell them," she pleaded.

"Well, you're NOT coming back with me." I said forcefully.

"I'm ok..... I really am.....Just let me drive home," she said insistently. Despite the lack of appreciation in her voice I was glad to hear these words.

"Did you really take anything?" I asked dryly. She didn't answer. We drove back to her car parked again behind the garages at the flat and I arranged to follow her down the motorway towards Chesterfield.

Quite by chance I arrived home just in time to look as though I'd just got up. A major confrontation with my parents had been miraculously avoided. Jenna waited out of sight whilst I had quick breakfast. Grabbing some bread for Jenna I left as though nothing had happened. Everything had gone unnoticed. Everything except I hadn't told my parents yet about being homeless. As I approached my car Jenna sat in readiness to drive off in front of me as arranged. I just hoped we wouldn't be spotted leaving together. We cleared the grounds of the flats area and entered the main road. I followed steadily behind as we negotiated the early morning traffic. I sat back in my seat and made myself comfortable. At last a moments peace. I began to think about my homeless state and where I was going to live and what I was going to tell my parents. Perhaps, I might find a place with Brian Whitworth from the band. He had recently moved into a place in Wickersley. It would be much more pleasant than the bedsit. Anything would be better than that place. With Brian I could control the problem of uninvited guests a little better. This thought brought me rapidly back to the same problem driving in the Hillman Imp in front of me.

"How was I going to stop her following me around?" I asked myself. "Just as you think she's had enough, she reappears." An injunction had been suggested but they were also difficult to administer. Nevertheless, perhaps this was the time to try this approach. I made my mind up, there and then, to approach a solicitor. As we drove down the middle lane of the motorway I stared at the profile of Jenna's head as she drove along in front of me. Everything seemed so calm now, sat here alone in the car. The feeling of relief was noticeable. During the last few days I'd almost forgotten what it was like. I began to think of the day's work ahead of me.

Then suddenly, without warning she leaned over and dropped from view. Vital seconds passed by. She didn't reappear. No one was at the wheel. I screamed inside.

"Where is she!" The car carried on ahead at about sixty miles per hour. At first the car hardly wavered from its course, steadily cruising along with ghostly persistence. But then it began a slow, but definite shift, to the left. It was only 7.30am and, at the moment, the motorway traffic was not too heavy. Instinctively I put my foot down hard on the accelerator pedal to try and catch her up.

"Jenna!" I shrieked, "Jenna!"

We were now travelling down a hill and she was gathering speed. The left side of the motorway lay open, without a barrier, and a steep drop lay in wait. If she went off there it would be certain disaster. I steered my minivan over to the left, all the time attempting to get on to the inside of her. My minivan was slow, so frustratingly slow. It was old and couldn't respond. Another car overtook me totally unaware of the incident in progress. I cursed the car for not having enough power. She was heading steadfastly for the edge, the nearside wheel entering on to the gravelly hard core of the service lane. I was almost certainly too late.

But then miraculously, her car began to change course and slowly steer itself back towards the centre. She crossed in front of me. This gave me a second chance.

On the hill, with my foot down, I was finally picking up speed and after a few more priceless seconds I managed to gradually pull along her nearside. As I glanced away from the road and into her car I still couldn't see any signs of Jenna. At that moment her car moved in towards me and there was a loud bang as her car hit the side of mine. She bounced off and now began a distinct shift towards the fast lane. A car behind hooted his horn loudly as he made an exaggerated gesture to get around us both. Her car came back again to hit me in the side, this time ricocheting off me into the central barrier of the motorway. She bounced back and forth, back and forth, off the barrier and into my car. The noise of crunching metal and breaking glass heightened the drama. It was terrifying. Other cars were now threatening to get in the way; the whole thing was about to escalate and get out of control. I persistently held on to this course; I was not going to let her go.

After a few more spine-chilling, seconds she was starting to slow down, there was hope but it wasn't over yet. About two hundred yards ahead a gap in the barrier threatened disaster again. She would almost certainly go straight through into the opposing traffic on the other side of the motorway or simply turn the car over.

"Jenna! Wake up!!" I shouted. It was a futile gesture. The sound of me shouting was totally drowned by the sound of our cars crashing together. I increased my speed to get in front. This time I made it. I could now see her car in my rear view mirror. I allowed her to catch up to the rear of the minivan. In this way I could perhaps bring her slowly to a halt. I waited for the moment as she struck the back of my car. By this time the cars had slowed down considerably so that the final impact was a relatively graceful affair. We continued a few yards further, her car continuing to noisily batter my rear. Finally, it was quiet. We had stopped.

But I could not continue to sit there. It was dangerous. We stood in the fast lane and the traffic continued to pass at high speed. I had to get out and get Jenna out. An immediate attempt to open my door failed. It was jammed tight. I scrambled over to the other side and attempted to open the passenger door into the direct flow of the traffic. Undaunted I pushed the door out further into the traffic just hoping for the best. A loud blast of a cars horn hit me as it sped past but I ignored it as I got out and ran to the other side of the car. I was astonished at the damage. Both my car and hers were wrecked. The side panels of the doors were a mess and couldn't be opened. I stared in through her car window. Jenna lay in a crumpled ball on the floor of the passenger side. She didn't move. I knocked furiously on the window and shouted to her but still she didn't move. I went around to the other side of the car. It was there to my horror I saw the true severity of the damage where the car had repeatedly hit the barrier.

"I've killed her!" I groaned, "I must have killed her." Suddenly, from out of nowhere a man appeared who wanted to help. He must have parked somewhere on the service lane. Calmly he generously offered his services. After only a brief and garbled explanation he spotted Jenna and realised what was to be done. He began to smash the remains of the door window and then wrench the door open. He squeezed himself in and then reached down towards her. It was then I saw her move.

"She's ok," he shouted. "She says she's ok." I tried to smile but no expression seemed appropriate to relieve the tension I felt. "Are you alright?" said the man concerned. I reassured him I was ok. He went to his car and, before returning, got out a red warning triangle and placed it on the road to steer away the oncoming traffic.
"You stay here with the girl. I'll go and get an ambulance."

The man, whoever he was, then disappeared as fast as he appeared. But I was thankful to him and that he cared enough to look after these matters. Jenna very slowly maneuvered herself on to the front passenger seat.

"Are you hurt?" She didn't look up but attempted to shake her head. I couldn't really hear anything as she tried to speak.

"He's gone to get an ambulance," I shouted, trying to reassure her.

All I could do now was wait for the ambulance. The cars continued to hurtle by as I rested my arms on the roof of her car. My breathing was still fast. Fortunately, it didn't seem long before the distinctive sound of a siren could be heard in the distance. The ambulance made a welcome appearance and parked in the service lane nearby. Jenna was wheeled across on a stretcher. The paramedics immediately asked me for an explanation of what had happened. I looked at them blankly. My expression must have said it all; it was impossible to begin. At their request, I accompanied her to the hospital and as we drove away, I took one final look at the motorway. The two tangled wrecks sat there, now motionless, locked together, as if frozen in eternal combat.

END OF PART ONE

Printed in Great Britain
by Amazon